D1201177

EARLY IN THE SUMMER ____________ OF 1970

By A. B. Yehoshua:

EARLY IN THE SUMMER OF 1970
THREE DAYS AND A CHILD

EARLY IN THE SUMMER OF 1970

A. B. Yehoshua

DOUBLEDAY & COMPANY, INC., GARDEN CITY, NEW YORK
1977

All of the characters in this book
are fictitious, and any resemblance
to actual persons, living or dead,
is purely coincidental.

Excerpt from "Redemption Through Sin" reprinted
by permission of Schocken Books Inc. from
THE MESSIANIC IDEA IN JUDAISM by Gershom Scholem.

"Early in the Summer of 1970" first appeared in *Commentary* magazine.

"Missile Base 612" first appeared in *Moment* magazine.

"The Last Commander" first appeared in *Present Tense* magazine.

ISBN: 0-385-02590-4
Library of Congress Catalog Card Number: 76-16262

Printed in the United States of America
First Edition

Contents

EARLY IN THE SUMMER OF 1970 — 7

Translated from the Hebrew by Miriam Arad

MISSILE BASE 612 — 73

Translated from the Hebrew by Miriam Arad

THE LAST COMMANDER — 131

Translated from the Hebrew by Pauline Shrier

Early in the Summer of 1970

I believe I ought to go over the moment when I learned of his death once more.

A summer morning, the sky wide, June, last days of the school year. I rise late, faintly stunned, straight into the depths of light; don't listen to the news, don't look at the paper. It is as though I had lost my sense of time.

I get to school late, search the dim green air in vain for a fading echo of the bell. Start pacing the empty playground, across squares of light and shadow cast by the row of windows, past droning sounds of classrooms at their work. And then, surprised, I discover that the Head is running after me, calling my name from afar.

Early in the Summer of 1970

Except that I have nearly arrived at my class, the Twelfth, their muffled clamor rising from the depth of the empty corridor. They have shut the door upon themselves not to betray my absence, but their excitement gives them away.

Again the Head calls my name from the other end of the corridor, but I ignore him, open the classroom door upon their yells and laughter which fade into a low murmur of disappointment. They had by now been certain I wouldn't show up today. I stand in the door waiting for them to sort themselves out, wild-haired, red-faced, in their blue school uniforms, scrambling back to their desks, kicking the small chairs, dropping Bibles, and gradually the desk tops are covered with blank sheets of paper, ready for the exam.

One of them is at the blackboard rubbing out wild words—a distorted image of myself. They look me straight in the eye, impudent, smiling to themselves, but silent. For the present my gray hairs still subdue them.

And then, as I walk softly into the room, the exam paper in my hand, the Head arrives, breathless, pale. All eyes stare at him but he does not even look at the class, looks only at me, tries to touch me, hold me; he who has not spoken to me for the past three years is all gentleness now, whispers, pleads almost: Just a moment . . . never mind . . . leave them . . . you've got to come with me. There's some notice for you . . . come. . . .

It is three years now that no words have passed between us, that we look at each other as though we were stone. Three years that I have not set foot in the common room either, have not sat on a chair in it, not touched the teapot. I intrude into the school grounds early in the morning, and during recess I wander up and down corridors or playground—summers in a large, broad-brimmed hat, winters in a greatcoat with the collar up—floating back and forth with the students. I pay my trips to the office long after school is out, leave my lists of grades, supply myself with chalk.

I hardly exchange a word with the other teachers.

Three years ago I had been due to retire, and had indeed resigned myself to the inevitable, had even considered venturing upon a little handbook of Bible instruction, but the war broke out suddenly and the air about me filled with the rumble of cannon and distant cries. I went to the Head to say I was not going to retire, I was staying on till the war would end. After all, now that the younger teachers were being called up one by one he would need me the more. He, however, did not see any connection between the war and myself. "The war is all but over," he told me with a curious smile, "and you deserve a rest."

No rest, however, but a fierce summer came, and flaming headlines. And two of our alumni, very young, killed one a day after the other. And again I went to him, deeply agitated, hands trembling, informed him in halting phrases that I did not see how I could leave them now, that is to say, now that we were sending them to their death.

But he saw no connection whatever between their death and myself.

The summer vacation started and I could find no rest, day after day in the empty school, hovering about the office, the Head's room, waiting for news, talking to parents, questioning them about their sons, watching pupils in army uniform come to ask about their matric grades or return books to the library, and sniffing the fire-singed smell in the far distance. And again, another death, unexpected, an older alumnus, much liked in his time, from one of the first class-years, killed by a mine on a dirt-track, and I at the Head again, shocked, beaten, telling him: "You see," but he straight away trying to brush me off: he has given instructions to prepare the pension forms, has planned a farewell party—which of course I declined.

A week before the new school year I offered to work for nothing if only he would give me back my classes, but he had already signed on a new teacher and I was no longer on the roster.

School starts. I arrive along with everyone in the morning, carrying briefcase and books and chalk, ready to teach. He spotted me near the common room and inquired anxiously what had happened, what was I doing here, but I, on the spur of the moment, did not reply, did not even look at him, as though he were a stone. He thought I had gone out of my mind, but in the turmoil of a new school year had no time to attend to me. And meanwhile my eyes had been searching out the new teacher, a thin, sallow young man, in order to follow him. He enters the classroom, and I linger a moment and enter on his heels. Excuse me, I say to him with a little smile, you must be mistaken, this isn't your class, and before he has time to recover I have mounted the platform, taken out my ragged Bible. He stammers an apology and leaves the room, and as for the dazed students who never expected to see me again, I give them no chance to say a word.

When after some moments the Head appears, I am deep in the lesson, the class listening absorbed. I would not budge.

I did not leave the room during recess, stayed planted in a crowd of students. The Head stood waiting for me outside but did not dare come near me. If he had I would have screamed, in front of the students I would have screamed and well he knew it; and there was nothing he feared as much as a scandal.

By sheer force I returned to teaching. I had no dealings with anyone but the students. For the first few weeks I scarcely left the school grounds, would haunt them even at night. And the Head in my wake, obsessed by me, dogs my steps, talks to me, appeals to me, holding, stroking, threatening, reproaching, speaking of common values, of good fellowship, of the many years of collaboration, coaxes me to write a book, is even prepared to finance its publication, sends messengers to me. But I would not reply—eyes on the ground, or on the sky, or on the ceiling; freezing to a white statue, on a street corner, in the corridor, in the empty classroom, by my own gate, or even in my armchair at home, evenings when he would come to talk to me. Till he gave up in despair.

He had meant to drag me into his office, but I did not wish to move out of the students' range. I walked a few paces out into the corridor and stopped, and before the attentive gaze of the students I wrung it all out of him.

Some five or six hours ago—

In the Jordan Valley—

Killed on the spot—

Could not have suffered—

Not broken it to his wife yet, nor to the university—

I am the first—

He had put my name on the forms and for some reason given the school for address.

Must be strong now . . .

And then the darkness. Of all things, darkness. Like a candle the sun going out in my eyes. The students sensed this eclipse but could not move, weren't set for the contingency of my needing help, whereas the Head talked on fluently as though he had been rehearsing this piece of news for the past three years. Till suddenly he gave a little exclamation.

But I had not fainted, only slumped to the floor and at once risen to my feet again, unaided, and the light was returning to me as well, still dim, in the empty classroom, seated on a student's chair, seeing people throng the room, teachers rushing in from nearby classrooms, curious students, office workers, the janitor, people who had not spoken to me these three years. Here they were all coming back, some with tears in their eyes, surrounding me, a whole tribe, breaking my loneliness.

He had returned from the United States three months ago, after an absence of many years. Arrived with his family late in the night, on a circuitous flight by way of the Far East. For six hours I waited at the airport, thinking at last that they wouldn't arrive, that I would have to go back as I came. But at midnight, when I was by then dozing on some bench in a corner, they approached me, emerged from the obscurity of the runway, as though not coming off a plane but back from a hike; rumpled and unkempt, heavy rucksacks on their backs and in one of them a white-faced toddler who looked at me with gentle eyes.

I hardly recognized my son in him. Bearded, heavy, soft, my son's hair was already sprinkled with gray, and, in his movements, some new, slow tranquillity. He, whom I had already given up for a lost bachelor, coming back a husband, a father, nearly a professor. I was dazzled by him. And he bringing his wife forward, in trousers, a slim girl, enveloped in hair, dressed in a worn-out tasseled coat, one of his students presumably; and then she is leaning toward me and smiling, her face clear. Very beautiful.

At that moment anyway I found her so beautiful, touching me with cool, transparent fingers.

And I, my heart overflowing, rise at once to touch them, kiss them, kiss the child at least, but he is too high for me, hovering up there in the rucksack, and as soon as I touch him he starts chattering English to me, and the thin student girl joins in as well, a shower of words, in two voices, pouring their incomprehensible English out over me. I turn to my son for illumination, and he listens with a smile as though he, too, could not take it in at first, then says they are amazed by the resemblance between us two.

And afterward the customs inspection, a long, remorseless affair, as though they were suspected of something, myself looking on from afar, watching all their parcels being taken apart. And when at last we embark on the journey home, in a dark taxicab, through a gradually lightening spring night, the baby is already drooping with sleep, like a plucked flower, huddled in his rucksack between the two of them on the front seat; while I, behind them, among the luggage, among a guitar, typewriter, and rolled-up posters, watch the loosely tied parcels softly disintegrate.

My son fell asleep at once, enfolding his sleeping son, but my daughter-in-law was surprisingly wakeful. Not looking out at the road, not at this land she had never seen, not at the stars or the new sky, but her whole body turned toward me sitting in the back, her hair tumbling over my face, she was shooting questions at me, speaking of the war, that is, what do people here say, and what do they really want, as though accusing me of something, as though in some furtive manner I were enjoying this war, as though there existed some other possibility. . . .

That or thereabouts, I mean, since I had much difficulty understanding her, I who was never taught English, and what I know is what I caught from the air, just so, from the air, from English lessons sounding out of adjacent classrooms when the hush of an examination is on mine, or when I pace the empty corridors waiting my turn to enter the class.

And I am straining to understand her, exhausted as I am from the long waiting hours in the night. And my sleeping son on the front seat, a heavy mass, his head wobbling, and I alone with her, observing the delicate features, the thin glasses she has suddenly put on, such a young intellectual, maybe this New Left thing, and for all that a trace of perfume, a faint scent of wilted flowers coming from her.

In the end I open my mouth to answer her. In an impossible English, a staggering concoction of my own make, laced with Hebrew words, lawless, and she momentarily taken aback, trying to understand, falling silent at last. Then, softly, she starts to sing.

And we arrive at my place, and though worn out they show the sudden efficiency of seasoned travelers, shed their sandals by the door and start walking about barefoot. Swiftly they unload their luggage and send the driver away. They pick up the sleepy child and quickly, both together, undress him, put him into some kind of sewn-up sheet like a little shroud and lay him on my bed. Then, as though suddenly discovering the immensity of their fatigue, they begin to undress themselves, right in front of me, move half naked through the small flat, and dawn is breaking. They spread blankets over the rug, and I glimpse her bare breasts, very white, and she sends me a tired smile, and all at once I lose my own sleep, all desire for sleep. I shut the door upon them and start wandering through what little space is still left me, waiting for signs of the sun itself. They had sunk into a deep sleep, and before I left for school I went and covered up their bare feet. At noon I returned very tired and found them still sleeping, all three of them. I thought I'd burst, I who was aching to talk to them. I had lunch by myself, lay down beside the child who was wet by now and tried to get some sleep, but could not. I got up and began to search through their luggage, see what they had brought, a book perhaps, or a magazine, but after a few minutes my hands flagged.

Toward nightfall I could bear their silence no longer. Softly I opened the door and came upon them. They lay slumped each to himself, submerged, catching up on the time they had lost in their journey round the world. Once again I bent down to cover my daughter-in-law's feet, but I turned back the blanket under which my son lay.

Little by little he awoke, naked, hairy, heavy, his breath catching, opened his eyes at last and discovered me in the half-light standing over him, looking down. He gave a brief start as though for an instant not recognizing me. "What's with you?" he whispered from the floor.

"At school still, every morning, the Head keeping silent still," I whisper at him in one breath.

For a moment he is puzzled, even though I used to write to him about everything, devotedly, all the details. Perhaps he did not read my letters. The silence grows, no sound except the breathing of the young woman by his side who has thrown off her blanket again. Little by little he recovers his composure, slowly pulls the blanket over himself. His eyes lift in a smile.

"And you're still teaching Bible there. . . ."

(Already he has nothing to say to me.)

"Yes, of course. Only Bible."

"In that case"—still smiling—"everything's as usual."

"Yes, as usual"—and another long silence—"except of course for my pupils getting killed," I spit out in a whisper straight into his face.

He shuts his eyes. Then he sits up, huddled in his blanket, his beard wild, picks up a pipe and sticks it into his mouth, begins to muse, like an ancient prophet, to explain that the war won't go on, haven't I noticed the signs, can't go on any longer. And now his wife wakes up as well, sits up beside him, likewise drapes the blanket about her, sends me a smile full of light, ready to make contact, join the conversation, explain her viewpoint, straight away, without going for a wash, coffee, her eyes still heavy with sleep, in the shimmer of spring twilight, in the littered room filled with their warmth.

Striding through the corridors to the office, a little mourning-procession, I in their midst, like a precious guest, like a captive. And classroom doors open a crack as though under the pressure of studies, and teachers' faces, blackboard faces, student faces, the entire school watching me as though discovering me anew.

. . . And we never knew he was back, you never told, your silence. I didn't think you'd remember him, though in fact he used to be a pupil here too. How old is he, was he? Thirty-one. God, when'll all this stop. So young. Not quite so young any more, took me aback when he got off the plane, aged some . . . And right away the Army take him? Give him no breathing-space? How no breathing-space, three months they gave him, everybody goes these days, and in the Six Day War he didn't take part, not before it either, and he's no better than everybody else, is he? But right away to the Jordan Valley? Yes, odd that, I never thought they'd still find a use for him, he himself was sure they'd send him to guard army stores in Jerusalem. . . .

And we cut across the empty playground simmering in the sun.

. . . And how about his wife. American, doesn't even know Hebrew. And whom has she got here? No one. And the child, how old is the child? A toddler still. About three. Oh, God Almighty, enough to make you cry. Who's going to be with them now? I'll be with them. . . .

And another corridor, classrooms, doors, and a flushed student in light-blue uniform running after us.

. . . What's up? Teacher left his briefcase and book behind in class. Oh, never mind, give here, I'll take them for him. What are you doing in there now? Nothing . . . I mean, waiting. . . . We're so sorry. . . . Maybe you could get on with that exam all the same? By ourselves? Yes, why not. . . .

And arriving at the office at last, heads bowed.

. . . Been years since I've set foot in your office. Yes, so pointless too, this breach between us, sit down a moment now, rest, a difficult time before you, I'm quite stunned myself, when they told me on the phone, I couldn't believe, would you like us to get in touch with the military now, maybe talk to them yourself. No, no need. Hadn't they better come here and pick you up, maybe let his wife know, the university. No, no need, I'll tell them all myself, I'll go to Jerusalem, I don't want anyone else to precede me. But that's impossible, you can't by yourself, must get in touch with the Army, they'll pick you up, someone must go to the hospital too . . . that is, to identify . . . you know . . . I'll identify him. Why're you getting up? What can we do for you? The entire school's at your service, say the word, what do you need? I need nothing, just to go, just want to go now. I'll take you, I'll come with you, it's madness for you to leave here by yourself, maybe somebody could drive you in his car. But why a car, I live so near, you're pressing me overmuch, I shall lose my breath again. . . .

But he insists on coming along. Abandons the school, his humming empire, and takes my arm in the street, carries my briefcase, the jacket, the ragged Bible. There are tears in his eyes, as though not my son but his had fallen. At every street corner I try to detach myself, that's enough, I say, but he insists on tagging on after me as though afraid to leave me alone. By my gate, under a blue morning sky, we come to a halt at last, subside like two large, gray, moss-grown rocks, and as a vapor above us trail the words of condolence that he does not believe in and I do not hear.

Finally silence, his last word spent. I collect my things from him, the jacket, Bible, briefcase, urge him to go back to the students, but still he refuses to take his leave, as though he had detected signs of a new breakdown in me, in my silence. And I put out my hand and he takes it and does not let go, seizes me in a tight grip, as though I had suddenly, mysteriously, gained a new hold over him, as though he would never be able to part from me again.

I leave him by the gate, go in and discover an unfamiliar kind of light in my flat, light of a weekday morning. I let down blinds (he is still standing by the gate), strip, and go to take a shower; knowing people will come close to me this day, touch me. Stand a long time naked under the streaming water, head throbbing, trying to tell his wife of his death in broken, water-swept English. Clean, cleanse myself, put on fresh linen, find a heavy black suit in the wardrobe and put it on. Peer through the blinds and see the Head still by my gate, rooted to the spot, sunk in thought, aloof, as though he had really given up his school. And then I tidy up the flat, unplug the telephone, let down the last blinds and all of a sudden, as though someone had given me a hard push, I fall down sobbing on the rug where they lay that night. And when I get up it is as though the darkness had grown. My temples ache. Softly I call to the Head who is there no longer, who is gone and has left the street empty, accessible.

And afterward supper, on the porch, on a spring evening filled with scents, under the branches of a tree in flower. And the three of them sit there, pink-cheeked, gorged with sleep, and I, very tired, knees trembling, bring them bread and water. They have brought out cans left from their travels and have spread a meal as though they were still on the road, a halt between inns. And the toddler still in his white shroud, sitting upright, clear-eyed, prattling endlessly, arguing with the crickets in the garden.

And my son is engrossed in his food, betrays a ravenous appetite, rummages among the cans, slices up bread, his eyes moist, and in vain I try to sound him out about his work, what exactly he is researching, what he intends to teach here, and has he perhaps brought some new gospel. He sits there and smiles, begins to talk, flounders, has difficulty explaining, doesn't think I'd understand him.

Even if he should give me stuff to read he doubts I'd be able to follow, the more as it is all in English. It is a matter of novel experiments, something in between history and statistics, the methods themselves such a revolution . . .

And he goes back to his food, his beard filling with crumbs, his head bent, chewing in silence, and I sink down before him, drawn to him, more than twenty-four hours without sleep, begin to speak to him softly, desperately, in a burning voice, about the endless war, about our isolation, about the morning papers, about the absent-mindedness of my pupils, about the bloodshed, about my long hours upon the platform, about history disintegrating, and all the time the child runs on, in non-stop English, babbling and singing, beating his knife on an empty can. And the night fills with stars, and my daughter-in-law, wide-eyed, restless, smiles at me, does not understand a word I say but nonetheless very tense, nodding her head eagerly. And only my son's attention wanders, the absent look in his eyes familiar, unhearing, already elsewhere, alien, adrift. . . .

And the night grows deeper and deeper, and every hour on the hour I open the radio to listen to the news, and the announcer's voice beats harsh and clear into the darkness. And my son swears at someone there who doesn't see things his way, then gets up and starts pacing the garden. And the child has fallen silent, sits bent over huge sheets of paper, painting the night, me, the crickets he has not seen yet. And my daughter-in-law at my side again, hasn't despaired of me and my English. She talks to me slowly, as if I were a backward pupil, her summery blouse open, her hair gathered at the back, a black ribbon encircling her forehead, all in all very much of a student still, of the kind that many years, eons ago, I might have fallen in love with, pursued in my heart, year after year.

And the night draws on, a kind of intoxication, dew begins to lap us. And she in a sudden burst of enthusiasm decides to sleep outside, fetches blankets from the house and covers up the child who has fallen asleep with his head on his papers, puts a blanket over me as well, and over her husband, and curls up in his lap, and he already puffing at his pipe, he who is thinking his own thoughts, whose heart there is no knowing, exchanges a few rapid sentences with her in English, kisses her with frightening intensity.

And I try to talk them into staying with me another day, but they cannot, must start getting organized, find a flat, a nursery school for the child, and I take leave of them, pick up the radio and go in, go to bed and fall asleep at once. And at daybreak, half in dream I see them load their bundles into a black cab, on their way to Jerusalem.

And without any preparations, without longing, like a bird, you too find yourself on the way to Jerusalem. On a bright morning, a Friday, on a fast, half-empty bus, among newspaper-rustling passengers, and no longer toiling up the old, tortuous road but tearing with a dull hiss through the widened valley, through trees that have receded, and there is no knowing any more whether one goes up to Jerusalem or down.

And suddenly you cry out, or think you do, and are amazed to see the people around you sink slowly into their tall seats, and for an instant the newspapers freeze in their hands. And you stand up, overcome, start crossing the aisle, and from the stealthy glances thrown at you you understand, they have made you out, you and your grief, but are powerless to help. And you want to vomit over the people, but they motion to the driver and he stops the bus, and you descend the iron steps into the roadside, near a painted yellow stripe, piles of earth and asphalt rubble, and you want to vomit over the view, over the mountains, the pines, but it comes to nothing, a fresh breeze plays about you, you recover your breath, and far away in the opposite lane cars rush past on their way to the Plain as on a different road. And you climb back into your bus, mumble apologies, and people look up kindly, say: That's all right. . . .

And shortly afterward on the Jerusalem hills, steeped in hard, hurting, almost impossible light, you make your way to the house of your dead son in an erstwhile border slum raised from the dust. Cobbled alleys have been paved over, ancient water holes connected to the drainage, ruins are turned into dwellings and in the closed courtyards new babies crawl. And you find the place at last, touch the ironwork door and it opens, and you lose your breath because the news has caught in your throat.

And softly you enter into an apartment turned upside down for cleaning, bunched-up curtains, chairs lifted onto tables, flowerpots on couch. Broom, dustpan, pail, rag, are strewn about the room. And the radio is singing Arabic in great lilting chorus and drums, heroic songs. And an Arab cleaning woman, very old, is wildly beating a red carpet. And his wife isn't there and the child is not. And your strength is ebbing, you stumble over the large tiles worn smooth by generations. And from great depths, through the loud singing, you try to dredge up forgotten Arabic words. *"Ya isma'i . . . el wallad . . . ibni . . . maath . . ."* (Listen . . . the child . . . my son . . . dead . . .)

Amazing that my cry does not frighten her, that she understands at once that I belong here, that I have rights, and perhaps she perceives traces of others in my features. Slowly she approaches me, the carpet-beater in her hand, an old crone (where did they dig her up?), her face crumpled, deaf apparently, for the radio is still going full blast.

Again I shout something, point at the radio, and she goes over to it at once, stoops by an elaborate device with multiple microphones, turns the knobs till the singing fades and only drums still rumble from some hidden microphone. Then she comes back to me, withered monkey, bent, swathed in skirts, her head covered with a large kerchief, waiting.

"Ibni . . ." I try again and fall silent, tears choke me, begin moving through the apartment, between upturned

chairs, dripping flowerpots, between cartons (still not unpacked), transformers, records, exploring amid this American clutter the apartment I never knew, and she in my wake, with the thudding drums, barefoot, still holding the carpet-beater, picking up things from under my feet, shifting chairs, letting down curtains, and increasing the confusion beyond repair.

And I reach the bedroom and find the bedclothes tumbled, long dresses strewn about, the imprint of her body on the sheet, the pillow; and in a corner still the invariable cartons, one atop the other.

The place will have to be arranged for mourning—

I sit on the bed, study the vaulting lines, begin to perceive the structure of the building, and the old woman by my side, imagines I ought not to be left alone, wishes to help me, serve me, expects me to lie down perhaps so as to cover me, and once more I try to explain very softly.

"*Ibni maath . . . walladi . . .*"

And finally she understands.

"*El zreir?*" (The little one?) she asks, as though I had many sons.

And I stand up, hopeless, try to send her away, but she has already grown attached to me, such faithfulness, my being such an old man perhaps, she awaits orders, apparently used to the fact that she will never understand what is said to her in this house, but totally overcome when she sees me begin to tidy up the room. Folding the bedclothes (discover a telephone between the twisted blankets and unplug it), spreading a rug over the bed, returning clothes to cartons and discover diapers in one of them, new, whole stacks of them in transparent wrappings, as though they planned to beget an entire tribe.

And in the next room still the beating drums—

And the old woman restless, fidgeting about me, wishing to help and not knowing how, begins to speak suddenly, or to sob, or scream, repeats the same phrase over and over, tirelessly, till I understand. She thought I had meant the child.

"*La, la, la zreir,*" (No, no, not little one). I lean toward her, breathing the scorched smell of dead bonfires in her clothes. "*Abuhu* . . ." (His father . . .)

But at that she seems ten times worse stricken:

"*Eish abuhu* . . . ?" (How, his father . . . ?")—stunned, unbelieving, taking a pace backward.

But I am seized with a sudden anxiety for the child, begin to look for him, want to fetch him home, and she grasps my intention at once, pulls me to the door, and on the doorstep, facing the little alleys, gesturing and yelling, she shows me the way to the nursery school.

And in a room swept with sun, smelling of bananas—the story hour; in a circle, upon tiny chairs, arms folded, all in blue pinafores, haven't identified him yet, all of them very still, listening tensely to the slow, confident, melodious voice of a little teacher. It is years since I have known so deep a silence among children, had not imagined them capable of it.

And dropping into this, me, in black, flushed, stepping

over piles of huge blocks, still trying to spot him, and something cracks in me, here of all places, and I wish to sink down beside the little towels hung up in a row, under the paintings scattered on the wall. And the brief shout of the teacher.

A bereavement in our family—

Before dawn—

But she, pale, misses the name, thinks I am rambling, thinks I belong at another nursery school perhaps, but then he stands up, rises like a slender stalk from his place, arms still folded, very grave, silently admits to the connection between us, listens to the teacher who has suddenly understood, has gone over to put her arms about him, addresses him in English, picks him up, lifts him out of the circle.

And at once the little lunch box is hung around his neck, a blue cap placed on his head, and he asks for something in his language and is immediately given a painting he has made that morning, and through the mist that veils my eyes I see—the page is filled with a red sun sparking splinters all around. And his little hand in mine, and my fingers closing over it. They have given him to me, even though I haven't told everything yet, could have been any old man entering a nursery school wishing to take away a child.

Back in their apartment. Soundless, barefoot, the Arab woman paddles about in the kitchen. The child is with her, eating an early lunch. Now and then a few soft phrases reach me, she talking to him in Arabic, he answering her in English. A distant rustle from the open windows. We are waiting only for her. Everything will be turned upside down here in a day or two, people will fill the rooms. In a month or two nothing will remain. She will stow the child in a rucksack and go back where she came from. I find his study, go in and shut the door upon myself. Dim and cool in here. Stacks of books on the floor, the desk littered with papers. Left everything as it was and went to the Army. Confusion of generations. I circle his desk, lightly touch his papers. Who could make order in this chaos. Fifteen years since I have inspected his exercise books. Vainly I try to let in some light. The blind has stuck, won't open. I come back to the desk. What had he been working on, what planned, and how can I link up with this. I touch the first layer and at once telephone bills, electricity bills, university circulars, come fluttering down. He is something of a teacher himself. I peel off a second layer—accounts, thick magazines in English, unfamiliar, pictures of men posturing for advertisements, some half naked, all of them long-haired, fat and lean revolutionaries displaying novel ties or striped trousers, small electric instruments of doubtful purpose. And suddenly I also find a pipe of his, and a smell of unknown tobacco. Tokens of my son's mystery. Son, child of mine. Another spell of dizziness. My eyes grow dim. I return to the window and strain all my powers to wrench the blind loose. Motes of light, a thin current of air; through the slats I discover a novel angle of a teeming wadi, and beyond it new buildings of the university. I return to my rummaging about the desk. Transcripts sent him by colleagues. Diagrams of statistical data. Will have to try and read these as well. Notes in his handwriting, book titles. Promises of new ideologies. I stuff some in my pocket. And now something genuinely his, a sheaf of papers in his handwriting, half in English, half in Hebrew, entitled "Prophecy and Politics." A new book perhaps, or an article. I pull drawers, perhaps there will be a personal diary as well, but they turn out to be almost empty. More pipes, a broken camera, old medicine bags, and snapshots of his girl-wife—by some trees, by a hill, a car, a river. And beyond the pictures, in a far corner of the drawer, I find a small knife, sharp, ornamented, inscribed with the word PEACE.

And the front door opens, and the house fills with the sound of light steps and with her laughter. The child's singsong, then the hectic whispering of the Arab woman. And now light streaming at me from the opening door. And she—in a light dress, still hot and sweaty from walking, her bag on her shoulder, sunglasses on her eyes, such a tourist. Stands there surprised at the depth of my intrusion, tries a smile for me at once, but I am buried in the chair, behind the desk, black-suited, heavy, the knife between my fingers.

She takes a few quick, airy steps toward me but suddenly she halts, has sensed something, dread seizes her, as though she had perceived the marks of death upon me.

"Something wrong—" her voice trembles, as though it

were I on the point of death, concealing a mortal wound beneath my garments.

And I straighten up, drop the knife, a burst of hot light hits me, begin to move, past her. Mumble the morning's tidings in an ancient, biblical Hebrew, and know—she will not understand, the words dart back at me. And am filled with pity for them, stroke the child's hair, incline my head before the old Arab woman, and am drawn onward to the hot light in the rooms, through the still open front door, toward the looming wadi, to the university. Will have to enlist their help.

And in a straight line, almost as the crow flies, I cross the wadi toward the university, and in a tangle of thicket, in the depth of a teeming ditch, for a moment I lose the sky. Suddenly I think of you and you alone, ardently, hungrily. My killed, mine only son. Out of the depths I cry, noon is passing, the Sabbath near, and in Jerusalem they still know nothing of your death. Your wife has not grasped the tidings. I was wrong, I should have let the authorities perform their duty.

And here rocks, and a very steep slope, and bushes growing out of an invisible earth tangling underfoot, and who would have imagined that near the university there could be such a wilderness still.

At last I have seen your papers. Vainly you feared that I would not understand, I understood at once, and I am inspired, burned and despairing of you. You came back to preach your gospel, I am with you, man, I have filled my pockets with your notes, shall learn English properly, shall go up into the mountains and wait for the wind.

And I crash through the barbed-wire fence surrounding the university, behind one of the marble buildings, a gnarled branch in my hand, a long time since I have been here, am confounded anew by the sequence of the buildings. Start looking for your faculty, wander along corridors, between oxygen bottles, dim laboratories, small libraries, hothouses, humming computers, and the campus emptying before my eyes, students receding.

And in the compound of the main library, defeated, I detain a last, book-laden, hurrying professor, but he has never heard your name and, embarrassed, he shows me the way to the offices. And a flock of clerks, just leaving, listen to me attentively, advise me that the telephones are disconnected already, that moreover they are not authorized to handle such tidings, perhaps I had better go to the police. And I realize suddenly: they take me for mad, or for some eternal student, a crank wishing to draw attention to himself. In a black suit, slightly earth-caked, and hands holding a branch. It is the branch that makes me so suspect.

And I throw it away at once, in the middle of the square, and hasten back to the faculty building, into a lighted, balcony-tiered lobby. And on the top landing a stout porter moves about, letting down blinds. I, from my depth down below, in a shout, ask him about you, and he *has* heard your name, knows you by sight at least. "That professor with the wild beard"—he says, and comes down to me, jangling his keys, and takes me up to your office at the end of a corridor. And on the door I find a long list of students who want to consult you, and near it a typed announcement of your absence due to reserve duty, and on one side a list of books that you are asking your students to read pending your return. And I turn all these papers over, combine them and write a first death notice, my dearly beloved. And the porter reads it over my shoulder and believes it straight away, brings me more thumbtacks to pin the paper to the door.

And we descend the stairs, and I tell him all about you, and our steps echo in the empty building. And the dusky light is pleasant, gentle to the eyes, I hang back, my steps waver, I would fain linger here awhile, but the porter is suddenly impatient, resolutely turns me out, back into the sun.

And it blazes with such passion, softening the world for a final conflagration. And I had said in my haste: early summer, and here it is high summer already. And back to drifting, in sweltering clothes, between the white buildings, the locked laboratories of the spirit, tramping across limp Jerusalemite grass, drawing, drawn, toward a lone remnant of American students sprawled on one of the lawns, abandoning themselves to the sun, barefoot, bearded, half naked some of them, nodding over copybooks and English Bibles, playing shriek-songs to themselves on small tape recorders. Calling me from afar—"You guy"—as though inviting me to accost them. And I do, I butt in, start winding among them, over them, step on their flabby, Diaspora limbs, strike at them lightly with the branch that has reappeared in my hand. I could have been appointed professor here myself if I had really been determined, couldn't I?

And far away, somewhere on the horizon—the Hills of Moab.

They laugh, so passive they are, maybe even slightly drugged, "You old man," they say to me, taking me for who knows what, for some waster, someone come to peddle drugs perhaps. They are pleased with me, "You're great," they say, twisting on the ground, wallowing in the sparse grass, no word of Hebrew they speak, only two days since they were set down at the airport. And I bend over them, am even prepared to examine them there and then, test their Bible knowledge, and I start talking to them in my broken, impossible English, which has all at once become intelligible to them.

"Hear me, children. My son killed in night. In Jordan. I mean, near the river," and I point at the horizon which is fading in a blue haze. And they laughing still, "Wonderful," they say, delighted, slap my back, eager to draw me in, make me join their crowd, assimilate me in the swelling beat of their song.

". . . I am grateful to you, my dear friend and Principal, for letting me address our students on this solemn occasion of their graduating from our school. I know, it wasn't easy for you to cede me this privilege for once.

You, after all, haven't given a single lesson for years, not stained your hands with chalk, not touched a red pencil to correct a paper. You no longer stand for hours in front of a class, for you are busy with the administrative part of education, the which you much prefer to any education proper. Nevertheless, and precisely therefor, you would always look forward impatiently to this moment when, before our anxious parents, you could hold forth as a guiding spirit to these youngsters; and all the more so in these troubled times.

"And who is not eager to address the young these days? We are all seized with a veritable passion for speaking to you, dear students, long-haired, inarticulate, slightly obtuse students, vague graduates without ideals, with your family cars, your discotheques and pettings at night in doorways. And with all that—with the strength and readiness to die. To burrow in bunkers for months on end, under constant fire, to charge at unseen wire fences in the night, so young, and in fact so disciplined, amazing us over and over with your obedience. Isn't that so, dear parents?

"Ladies and gentlemen, I am not speaking to you as senior teacher, but as one who was a father and is so no more. I came here the way I am and you see me with my beard of mourning, my dark clothes. I have no message, but I want to encourage you. See, I too have lost a son, though he was not quite so young any more. We thought he would go to guard army stores in Jerusalem, but they sent him to the Jordan Valley. Thirty-one years old. An only, beloved son. Dear parents, students, I do not want to burden you with my grief, but I ask you to look at me and guard yourself against surprise, because I was prepared for his death in a manner, and that was my strength in that fearful moment.

"And even on that very Friday I was informed of his death, before going to identify him, very lonely, wandering across lawns, between university buildings, under a fierce sun, even then I began to think of you, of the things I should say to you, how out of my private sorrow a common truth would illumine us all. . . ."

From a great distance, beyond the summer clouds, as from a bird's-eye view, I look down upon myself. A tiny speck, abandoning the pale cubes and rolling slowly through a great splash of asphalt. An intersection. And all about—the heart of the dominion, a pile of government offices, reddish Parliament, sheer white museum, pine trees like soft moss, nibbled hills, blasted rocks, ribbons of road one atop the other—a plain attempt to transform the scenery. And a black dot comes spewing smoke from the east, stops beside the speck and swallows it.

It is an old taxi, some charred relic, and I drop onto torn and sweaty upholstery and wave the driver on.

Southward. Through the stifling air—the stubbornness. Cemetery Hill, twisted lines of graves as a wild scrawl, and on all sides still more buildings, big housing projects, scaffolds, cranes, like rocket pits. Houses copulating with houses. The Kingdom of Heaven by force of stone.

And the driver—an unshaven ruffian, ageless, cracking sunflower seeds, hums under his breath, peers at me constantly through his mirror, ready for contact.

But I shut my eyes.

The taxi worms its way down the slope to a wadi, leaving a thick trail behind it. The hospital comes into view. A red rock dropped there once and turned into a windowed dam, hushed in the midday air, a small helicopter hovering above like a bird of prey.

My clothes are shedding wisps of grass. I doze, dream. The car rattles, its doors shake, windows subside. The hum of the springs sends the driver's spirits soaring and, having given me up, he starts singing aloud, with abandon, vigorously banging his steering wheel.

But I am transcending the heights, dominating the view. Long wadis drawing from Jerusalem to Mount Hebron, pouring, delving into bare eternal hills. Olive groves, stone fences, flocks of sheep, the beauty of it, ancient kingdom changeless for thousands of years, and in the same glance, higher up, the sea appears and the mouth of the desert. Heavily does this fearful land seize me by the neck.

I touch the back of the driver's neck lightly, his singing is cut short at once. I begin to talk. He does not understand at first, thinks I have gone out of my mind. But over the short distance remaining us to the hospital I manage to convey the essential.

Yes, at thirty-one—

Only son—
Before dawn—

They were expecting me, as indeed they had said this morning, in the heart of the tiled compound, in the heart of the mountains, an army chaplain, heavy-limbed, his beard red and savage, a khaki-clad prophet, stands with the sun in his eyes, waiting. And when I arrive in my taxi he spots me at once, as though bereavement had marked me already, hurries to catch me before I should vanish through one of the glass doors gaping on all sides.

"You the father?"

"I am the father."

"Alone?"

"Alone."

He is astounded. His eyes burn. How on earth? How could they have let you come alone? For it isn't merely a matter of identification but a last leavetaking as well.

I know, but have no answer. Only cling to him with speechless fervor. At last a real rabbi, a man of God at my disposal. And silently I attach myself to his sweat-stained clothes, lightly touch his officer's insignia, and he, surprised at my clutching hands, surprised too at my weakness stirring at him through my hot clothes, puts his arm about me in embarrassment, his shoulders sag, tears in his eyes, and slowly, in the same embrace, he turns me toward the sun's radiance pouring out of the west, and softly pulls me inside.

Into an enormous and empty elevator, and at once we

sink slowly to the depths, no longer touching each other now, he beside the panel of buttons, I in a far corner, an empty stretcher between us.

He listens, his head tilted, his face blank, eyes extinguished; I am apparently talking again, not listening to myself, mechanically, probing the pain, the words happening far away, on some vague horizon, words already spoken several times today: thirty-one years old, nearly professor. Only son. Though saw little of him these past few years. A matter of months since he came back from the United States, grown a beard, hardly recognized him. Beloved son. Now he is leaving a wife, American, young, obscure. Leaving me a child. Leaving manuscripts, unfinished researches, cartons scattered through his house, leaving wires and transformers. Enough to drive one mad. Our children getting killed and we left with things . . .

I am still speaking of him as though he were far away from me, lying in some desert somewhere, as though he weren't a couple of yards away, as though I weren't moving toward him in a slow but certain falling, which is arrested at last with a soft jolt that kindles the chaplain's eyes anew. Automatically the doors tear open before us—

He takes hold of me. I must have shown signs of wanting to escape. Leads me through lighted corridors of a basement filled with the breathing of engines. At the crossings, between corridors, sudden gusts of wind blow at us. In a little cabinet people rise to meet us, doctors, officials, bend their heads when they see me enter, close their eyes for an instant. Some retreat at once, begin to slip away, some are, on the contrary, drawn toward me, want to touch me. The chaplain whispers: "This is the father who's come alone," and I, terrified, start mumbling again, the familiar formula. And someone at once steps nearer to listen, and a hush all around.

There is a wonderful gentleness in their attitude toward me, in the way they place me in a chair, put a skullcap on my head, in the swiftness with which they extract the identity card from my clothes, write something down, open a side door; and when they help me up I seem weightless, drawn floating by their hands into a vault, a bare concrete floor, screens everywhere, beating of white wings.

I shiver—

There is an unmistakable sound of flowing water in the room, as though springs were bubbling up in it.

The shed blood—

The child. This curse fallen upon me.

Someone is already standing beside one of the screens, draws a curtain aside, turns the blanket back, and I still afar, swept by a dreadful curiosity, my breathing faint, fading, heart almost still, slip out of the hands holding me, glide softly, irresistibly over there, to look at the pale face of a dead young man, naked under the blanket, at thin lines of blood circling blank half-open eyes. I shrink back slightly, the skullcap slips off my head.

A deep hush. Everyone is watching me. The chaplain stands motionless, his hand in his waistcoat, any moment now he will come out with a ram's horn, blow us a feeble blast.

"It isn't him. . . ." I whisper at last with infinite astonishment, with growing despair, with the murmur of the water flowing in this damned room.

Someone switches on more light, as though it were a question of light. The silence lasts. I realize: no one wants to understand.

"It isn't him," I say again, say without voice, without breath, gasping for air, "you must have made a mistake. . . ."

Amazement comes to them at last. The chaplain attacks a scrap of paper tied to the stretcher, reads the name aloud.

"Only the name is right. . . ." myself still in a whisper, and I retreat, and in the deep silence, the murmur of water flowing unseen, the sweet smell of decay, return to the little cabinet which has already grown to be my oasis.

Behind my back the chaplain begins to swear at someone and the little group collapses.

Friday afternoon, and though I see neither sun nor mountains, I know—we are on the outskirts of town, deep in the vaults of a hospital that leans heavily into a wild plunging wadi. The people around me want to go home, the nearer the Sabbath the farther the town draws away from them. They had been waiting for me in patience, knowing how brief the ceremony, a few seconds—enter, look, weep, part; sign a paper too perhaps, because somewhere the evidence must be left. I am not the first to come here after all, nor the last.

Now I am keeping them back. How distressing therefore to see the people enter the room with eyes lowered as in guilt. And when they see me sitting in a corner words fail them. Such a terrible mistake. And behind the walls I hear the whirring of bells, frantic telephones. They are trying to sort out the confusion before I should start fanning false hopes.

But I am not fanning a thing. Only straighten up suddenly and stand on my feet, watching the others in silence. It is only a truce, I tell myself, a little cease-fire. But they are dismayed at my rising, believe I am going violent on them, are already resigning themselves to it, except that I am nothing of the kind, only start moving slowly and dazedly about the room, from wall to wall, and, like a dog, find a plate in some corner with a few stale biscuits on it, take one and start munching. I have eaten nothing since this morning.

But it sticks in my throat at once, as though I were chewing dust or ashes, dust mingled with ashes.

I vomit–

At last–

They had been waiting for this, had been prepared. Used to it apparently. They sit me in a chair at once, clean up, offer me some smelling salts.

"It wasn't my son. . . ." I mumble at them with a face drained of blood.

Again the chaplain appears, looking very somber, his

eyes glowing, desperate, his beard unkempt, cap awry, the badges on his shoulder shining, invites me in a low voice to return to the room of the murmuring water.

Now I am faced with three screens. The light is glaring, they have turned it full on, thinking again that it is a question of light, that it is with light they'll convince me. Never has such a thing happened to them, and they suspect some fearful muddle may be at the bottom of it. And again I stagger, the shed blood. My son. This curse. And again my breathing grows faint, fades, heart still. Glide softly from stretcher to stretcher, lost faces, young men, like faces in my class, only the eyes closed, slightly rolled upward.

Not him–

They take me back to the first stretcher again, as though they were really resolved to drive me out of my mind.

"I'm sorry. . . ." I falter and collapse against the chaplain, against the open water channels running along the walls that my eyes detect at last.

I believe I must go over the moment when I learned of his death again.

Summer morning, the sky torn wide from end to end, June, last days of the school year. I rise late, languid, faintly stunned, unaware of time, straight into the glare of light.

Climb the school steps after the bell has faded. An echo still lingers among the treetops, in the dim green air. Start pacing through the emptying corridors, among last stragglers hurrying toward classrooms, make my way slowly for my Twelfth, from afar already sense their nervousness, their restive murmur.

Those huddling in the doorway spy me from afar and curse, hurry inside to warn the others. A last squeal of the girls. I by the door, and they tense and upright by their chairs, the white sheets of paper spread on their desks like flags of surrender, Bibles shelved deep inside.

The tyranny I enforce by means of the Bible—

Each examination takes on a fearful importance—

I greet them, they sit down. I call one of the girls and she comes over, long-haired, delicate, wordlessly receives the test papers, passes softly between the rows distributing them. The silence deepens, heads bend. The frozen hush and excitement of the first rapid survey.

I know: it is a hard test. Never before have I composed such a cruel text.

Slowly they raise their eyes. Their faces start to burn, a dumb amazement seizes them. They exchange despairing glances. Some of them raise their fingers at me, standing over them high on my platform, but I mow them down with a gesture of my hand. They are stunned, fail to see my purpose. They cannot utter a word before I silence them. Each of them forlorn in his seat. And suddenly, as though it were light they lacked, someone gets up and pulls the curtains, but to no avail. The new light trickling in at them only exasperates them the more. They try writing something, nibble their pens, but give up, a few already tearing up the papers. Someone rises and leaves the room with flaming face. Another follows, and a third, suddenly it seems as though they were up in revolt. At last.

And at that moment the quick steps of the Head sound, as though the rumor had reached him. He opens the door and enters, very pale, out of breath, does not look at the class but makes straight for me, mounts the platform, takes hold of me, three years that we haven't spoken and suddenly he clasps me to him hard, before the astonished eyes of the pupils. Whispers at me: Just a moment . . . leave them . . . never mind . . . come with me. . . .

One possibility—not to insist. To release these people, give them time; not to struggle against the waning sun, let the Sabbath descend upon Jerusalem in peace, let the rabbi reach home in time. And for the time being sever contact, depart, come down from the mountains, arrive in the evening, steal softly through our shadowy street. Enter the house through the back door, undress, not think, not tell, wait, the telephone disconnected, the door locked. To make the bed, try to sleep; and wait for a new, more authoritative call.

A second possibility—to insist, shout, tear clothes. To assail the chaplain, the others, demand immediate proof. To rout out additional people, organize a search party. A procession through the streets of Jerusalem on the Sabbath eve, wandering from one hospital to the next, to comb the cellars, descend into hell, find him.

Another possibility—not to stir. Do nothing. Go on

lying on this stretcher, covered with a blanket, in this hospital, in the little cabinet. There, someone is already holding a glass of water to my lips.

I open my eyes. It is the chaplain, wild and woebegone prophet, surrounded by doctors, gives me to drink with his own hands and with infinite tenderness.

He feels they owe me some explanation—

But he has none.

Groping in the dark.

Has no words even.

Nothing like it ever happened to him.

The people here are baffled as well.

Something very deep has gone awry—

Telephone calls will solve nothing, he knows. What ought to be done is to go back to sources: to the brigade, the battalion, maybe to the company itself.

My suffering is great, but who knows, perhaps out of it a new rising may come.

He had not wanted to use that expression, it is too big. He is very much afraid of false hopes.

There is a wonderful *midrash*, full of wisdom, only loath to trouble me now.

Such violent times, appalling—

Runs from one funeral to the next.

Nights sits at home amending funeral orations—

And he bends over me: to stay here, on this stretcher, rolled up in a blanket, serves no purpose. We ought to go to Jerusalem—

If possible before the onset of the Sabbath—

Suggests therefore that I collect myself, that is, if I still have some strength left. That I remove the blanket, get off the stretcher. They won't leave me to wander about by myself any more.

Incidentally, my status is dubious from the point of religious law as well—should my garment be rent or not. However, to be on the safe side, to ward off illusions, and again, before Sabbath sets in—

And he takes a small penknife out of his pocket, removes my blanket, and as I lie there, everyone watching, he makes a long tear in my dress.

And we start the ascent, out of the depths, in the same elevator and at the same slow speed, stumble out into the same compound and find a different light, different air, signs of a new hush. And climbing up out of the wadi, out of the heart of the mountains, and with us the sun, caught on the roof of the chaplain's small military car. He is driving zealously, sounding his horn to high heaven, his beard blowing, the steering wheel digging into his stomach, hurtles between near-empty buses, trying to overtake the Sabbath, which is descending upon him from the hazy eastern sky.

There is something desolate about the summery streets of Jerusalem vanquished by the Sabbath's might. I think of my house, of our street at this hour, decked in greenery, with a heavy perfume of blossoming, a swish of cars being washed, and the water murmuring along the curb.

And a taste of autumn suddenly, clouds caught in pines

and cypresses. And we burst at a gallop into a large, empty military camp scattered through a grove on a hill, and just at that moment the Sabbath siren rises from the town like a wail. The chaplain stops the car at once, kills the engine, drops his hands off the wheel, listens to the sound as though he were hearing some new gospel, then goes to find someone from brigade staff.

But there is no one, only barracks with boarded-up windows, stretches of cracked and barren concrete, and small yellow signs with military postbox numbers. The Army has migrated to the firing lines and left only white-washed skeletons behind, and legends on blank walls: COMPANY A., MESS, Q.M., SYNAGOGUE.

And torn, sagging wire fences, and weeds rustling underfoot, and I still trailing behind the chaplain who circles the barracks, knocks on imaginary doors, recedes from view, is lost and reappears, his beard shining through the trees.

And I, who never served in the Army, and in the War of Independence only stood beside road barriers, double up at last upon a rock in the center of a crumbling parade ground, the torn flap dangling on my breast, and the smell of ancient hosts about me.

Such despair—

Since morning I have been rolling down an abyss.

This sad hush around me.

And then, as though sprung from the soil, people collect round me, hairy half-naked soldiers, their shoelaces untied, carrying towels and tiny transistors purring Sabbath songs, weary drivers emerging from one of the barracks on their way to the shower. They surround me silently in the middle of the parade ground, and once again I, gray and tired, with the same story: Thirty-one. Informed of his death this morning. Lecturer at the university. Left a wife and child. They know nothing yet. Myself come to Jerusalem to identify him, and then find—it's not him. . . .

Their amazement—

The towels crumple in their hands—

How not him?

Not him. Not his body. Someone else.

Who?

How should I know?

And what about him?

That's what I'm asking. Maybe you know someone who could help.

They tremble. Something in the story has shaken them, hairy men with towels and soap dishes, they silence the transistors at once, forget about their shower, take my arms and pull me up, supporting me, cursing the Army. Never in their life heard of such a thing happening. It looks as though they would like to beat somebody up, some officer perhaps. And one of them recalls having seen the jeep of the brigade Intelligence officer under a tree somewhere, and at once they take me there. And in a coppice, beneath foliage, beside a locked barrack-turned-storehouse, the jeep stands, loaded with machine guns and ammunition, its front wheels grazing one of the doors. They try to break down the door but fail, break through a window and peer into a dim room filled with ammunition boxes. And in the corner a camp bed. Someone vaults into the room and wakes up a boy in khaki, a lean officer, curled up like a foetus, in his clothes, shoes, revolver on his thigh, fallen asleep amid the explosives.

He wakes up at once, opens his eyes and waits. They tell him breathlessly, shouting, pointing their fingers at me rooted outside, by the window, like a frozen picture. But he does not look at me. Sits bent over on the bed in his crumpled clothes, indifferent to the general excitement. And only when the confusion of voices dies down, and the wind whispering in the pines is suddenly heard, does he begin to talk to me from afar in a slow, quiet voice.

What's your name?

I give it.

What's his?

I give it.

And it's not him.

Not him.

Who brought you here?

The chaplain.

His eyes darken, a lengthy silence, and at last very softly:

And what do you want?

To find him . . .

He makes no response, as though fallen asleep again. Then he gets up, tired, dream-wrapped, but suddenly assuming the airs of a general, folds up the blanket, opens the door which he had barred upon himself from within, goes out and vanishes among the pines, into their soft whisperings. The drivers follow, find him by a rusty tap half buried under a drift of dead pine-needles, holding his head under it and letting the cool water splash over him. Then he steps aside, not looking, letting the drops trickle. Now the drivers are really ready to hit him. But with the water drying, his eyes quickening, his head bent, he has made up his mind already, and in a quiet voice starts giving out commands to the drivers. He sends one of them to find the wandering chaplain, orders another to bring the jeep around and fill it up, and the rest have already seized me, lifted me, as though I were paralyzed. They clear a place for me in the jeep and wedge me in between a greasy machine gun, cartridge cases, and smoke shells, place a helmet on my gray hairs, and firmly secure the strap around my chin.

And someone switches on the field radio by my side and it stirs into life with a thin shriek. And as though of its own accord, so slow as to be imperceptible, the jeep begins to move, surrounded by drivers half pushing it, half tagging in its wake. And from somewhere, at the last minute, they have fetched back the chaplain as well, sweat-drenched, lost, burnt out, dreaming of his Sabbath, and he too joins the slow procession, lagging a little behind. Notices me driven off, sitting pinioned between machine guns, and is unamazed. They are taking me away from him and he yields me up, is even ready to give his blessing to the journey. What's to be done? He has found no one at staff quarters, tried to get in touch with front staff and failed. But has left instructions behind, written out the full story.

And still he trudges behind the slow jeep, through the trees, the humming of the field radio. What else? What else is bothering him? It appears that something has turned up after all, the dead man's personal file, lying on some table. And a sudden thought strikes him—maybe it's all a mistake, maybe only the name is identical but it's not my son. And maybe it would be well if, at the last moment, before going down into the desert, I took a glance at the picture at least. And he pushes a brief khaki folder into my hands, and the men crowd around to look at it with me. And I open it to the first page and find the picture of a thin boy, just out of high school, fifteen years back, my son, in khaki shirt, cropped hair, looking at me with obstinate eyes.

The time is half-past five in the afternoon. A tall aerial scratches the last of the sun. A hesitant jeep is crossing Jerusalem as though in search of a missing person, someone to obviate the purpose of its journey, and meanwhile a Jerusalemite orange-red Sabbath is trampled under dusty wheels.

Passersby stop to gaze at the elderly civilian, dressed in black, helmeted, his eyes red with weeping. There is something in the way I grip the machine gun that poses a menace for the Jerusalemites—the Jews in its western half first, then the Arabs; as though I intended to mow them down, I who do not even know where the trigger is.

I ask the little officer.

He shows me—

I finger it—

(So tiny.)

And then the final collapse of the Sabbath beyond East Jerusalem, the last signs of green dissolving, and the stark white of bare stone houses, of pale, powdery soil at the roadside, bluish smoke from invisible fires in courtyards, and near them Arabs, glancing up and away from us.

And then another collapse, of the road itself, toward a gray, sunless desert appearing beyond a bend in a setting of smoky clouds.

At last, my solemn and fully armed entry into the Jordan Valley, where I have never yet set foot.

And to look at once for signs of a dead, distant, biblical deity among the arid hills flanking the road, in the sun-cracked face of an elderly soldier lifting the barrier.

And from here, I have been waiting for this, I knew, I knew, a great burst of speed, a resurgence. The jeep spins forward, and the officer, as though wrestling with someone, his lips set tight, eyes narrowed, starts driving wildly, greedily. And I cling to the gun in the face of a great sweeping wind, thrust my hand into my clothes and start weeding out papers—bus tickets, old receipts, lists of students, notes from my son's desk, the draft of a speech, text of the morning's examination.

And then, at last, the Army proper, and in the falling light. The sad, pellucid desert light dying over a camp of tents, barracks, tanks and half-tracks and immense towering aerials, and smoke spiraling from a chimney as though a different kind of Sabbath reigned here. And old, scorched soldiers in outsize overalls opening still another barrier before us, as though the desert were carved up by barriers.

People crowd around us—

They had been expecting us—

They even run after the jeep.

"The old father's arrived," someone shouts, as though I were a sacred figure.

And before long they have unloaded me, detached me carefully from the machine gun, loosened the cartridge belt that has coiled itself about me, dislodged a bullet which I have inserted into the barrel by mistake, and lower me, dusty and old, the helmet askew, lead me in the gathering darkness to their commanding officer.

And suddenly, deep in the distance, beyond the hills, shots resound.

My heart freezes—

Such warmth in the touch of their hands on my body, their gladness that a really old man has come among them, in a helmet, a civilian dimension in their desert night, that they dare blurt in an initiatory whisper as were it a sinful thought: "He's not been killed," "It isn't him," "You've been misled. . . ."

But the commander's voice asserts itself, carries firmly through the new darkness, and without seeing his face, listening to a voice heard before sometime, an old pupil doubtless, I nearly identify the voice, impossible that I should not–

. . . The encounter happened at night and the body was transferred to hospital before dawn. The men hardly know each other. Some of them haven't been with the unit for years. The clerk was only given an identity tag to go by, and from that set the chain of documents moving. He never looked at the dead man's face. They had taken everything to be in order, and then they received a phone call from headquarters in Jerusalem a short while back, someone giving them the whole story, saying we were on the way. And at once they had put their entire radio network into action. The men are scattered over a huge area. They inquired about the name right away, was there anyone answering to this name, and then, just a while back, someone was found. A man of thirty-one, from Jerusalem. And his military number too, corresponding to that of the body's. That is, the tags must have got shuffled somehow. And they'll still have to get to the bottom of that. Anyhow, they asked no more questions, did not want to alarm him, tell him his family had already been informed. But they are certain it is my son. Bound to be. And so long as I'm here, maybe I'd better see him with my own eyes after all. That way everybody's mind will be at ease. And better before the night is through. Look, he's with the patrol, they'll be here soon, and they've already arranged for them to be waiting at a little distance from here, so if I've come as far as this . . . the forward position . . . maybe I'd go on just a bit farther . . . that is, if I have the strength. . . . Here, get up on this armored car. . . . The word had got down from command about my pluck, considering. . . .

And suddenly it strikes me. He is afraid of me. This silence of mine, the endless patience, the way I stand there facing him, limp, demanding nothing; the passiveness with which I still wear the crushing helmet on my head. Something has gone wrong within his sphere of command and he is alarmed by the tyranny of my silence.

And again, from the distance—long volleys, strung out, echoes splintering.

This time it is a heavy half-track they take me to. They open an iron door, install me, seal the armored slits. Two or three soldiers clamber up and position themselves beside the machine guns, someone bends over the field radio and starts muttering.

With infinite slowness, with extinguished lights, tracks churning, cooped in an iron hutch dark except for the glimmer of a tiny red bulb—I understand. We are returning to the Jordan, they want to send me over to the other side, take me out unto the source. All that has happened has but been a prelude.

And suddenly we stop. The engine falls silent. Someone

lowers himself and opens the iron door from without, releases me. A junction of dirt tracks, desert and yet not-desert, reeds and shrubs in a narrow ditch beside the road. And silence, no shooting, and a light breeze, and a star-studded sky. We wait. Crouched low upon stones beside the track, in the thicket. And once again I find myself delivered into new hands. Someone not young and not old. An intelligent, sympathetic face, watching me intently, smiling. Something about me seems to amuse him, the helmet perhaps, I attempt to pry it loose. The smile persists. It turns out to be my age that bothers him.

"Seventy years old."

Sabbath eve. Matches flicker on the half-track, cigarettes are lighted. The soldiers are talking in low voices, cursing softly, calculating the number of Sabbaths still left them here. The field radio splutters feebly, someone distant signaling, "Can you hear me? Hear me?" but no one takes the trouble to reply.

What do I do?

I tell him.

He smiles. He had thought as much.

"It's my Hebrew," I say quietly.

What about it?

"Some rhetoric still left perhaps."

No, he smiles, not at all, but the eyes, the expression in them. He used to have a history teacher with just the same look.

"What history?"

"Jewish history."

"And he looked like me?"

"Yes."

"Despite the difference."

"What difference?"

"Between history and Bible."

"Why difference?"

And I rise, the torn flap drops from my heart, begin to explain with quiet fervor.

". . . I am coming to the main point of my speech. All this has been nothing but a prelude. Mr. Principal, colleagues, ladies and gentlemen, dear students, forgive me but I feel the need to say a few words to those among us who may disappear.

"On the face of it, your disappearance is nothing, is meaningless, futile. Because historically speaking, however stubborn you are, your death will again be but a weary repetition in a slightly different setting. Another tinge of hills, new contours of desert, a new species of shrub, astounding types of weapon. But the blood the same, and the pain so familiar.

"Yet another, other, glance reverses it all, as it were. Your disappearance fills with meaning, becomes a fiery brand, a source of wonderful, lasting inspiration.

"For to say it plainly and clearly—there is no history. Only a few scraps of text, some potsherds. All further research is futile. To glue oneself to the radio again and again, or seek salvation in the newspapers—utter madness.

"Everything fills with mystery again. Your notebooks,

your chewed pencils, each object left behind you fills with longing. And we who move in a circle behind you and unwittingly trample your light footsteps, we must be vigilant, as in a brief nightly halt in the desert, between arid hills, upon barren, unmurmuring soil. . . ."

And then out of the vastness a murmur rises, and from the east or west or north—I for one have lost my bearings—the patrol arrives, shining in a cloud of dust, two or three armored vehicles, with growing clatter, in the dark, now and then sending a strong beam of light at the embankment, then brandishing it about the arid hills, at the sky.

And there, in that booming clatter, my son must be too. A thirty-one-year-old private whose desk is littered with drafts for researches is now stuck in a half-track, beside a machine gun or mortar, flashing a beacon upon me and aiming his barrel at me.

Their beam hits us—

Someone fires a shot in our direction.

They have forgotten who we are, take us for infiltrators—

Only everyone shouts at once with all their might.

They would have killed us—

They pull up at some distance, two half-tracks and a tank, engines roaring, and the valley stirs into life. Vague nightly shapes, faces indiscernible. The officer beside me goes to look for the man in charge. And I, in my darkness, planted on my spot, scan the dim silhouettes and suddenly give up, convinced it is all for nothing, tremble in every limb, am ready to admit to the first identification.

A few soldiers jump off to urinate on the chains, and all of a sudden I discover him too, heavy, long-haired, sleep-walking, lonely, he too urinating.

Myself unseen I make no move, watch him from afar; know, his linen must be foul. As a boy he would come home like that from any hike of a day or two, as filthy as if he had crossed a desert.

Meanwhile they have located him. The commander calls his name. He turns, does up his buttons, comes over, a lumbering shape. Strange, he is not surprised to find me, his old father, late in the evening, in a helmet, a few paces from the river Jordan.

Two officers take hold of him. The half-track engines fall silent. And suddenly a deep hush.

"This him?"

"Yes." I touch him lightly.

He smiles at us, his beard ragged, understanding nothing, very tired, stands before me hung about with grenades, the rifle dangling from his shoulder like a broomstick.

"What's happened?"

How explain it to him.

"Anything wrong at home?"

How tell him that I had already given him up, intruded into his room, ruffled his papers, that I had planned to collect them for a book.

"You were reported killed. . . ."

Not I, someone else said that.

He does not understand, how could he, stooping a little under his kit, his helmet pushed back, his face inscrutable, his eyes holding me, like his son's eyes, like mine gazing at him. This is how he would look at me when he was small, when I would beat him.

He is asked to show the tags–

Gradually a crowd of soldiers is piling up about us.

He starts hunting through his pockets with surprising meekness, takes out bits of paper, shoelaces, rifle bullets, white four-by-two flannel, more flannel, sheds flannel like notes, but the tags fail to turn up. Lost them. Though they were tied to his first-aid dressing.

"Where's the dressing?"

Gave it to the medic after the encounter. It follows that he gave the tags as well. I begin to suspect that he, too, had considered disappearing, here beside the Jordan, or perhaps he just wanted to signal to me.

The medical orderly is summoned–

Out of the darkness they fish up a scraggy little fellow, middle-aged, embittered, smoking hungrily, who does not remember a thing. Yes, some people gave him their dressings, but he doesn't know about tags. Found tags on the dead man and put them around his neck. Was useless dressing him anyway. Halfway through had realized the man was dead. Finished the job anyway. No, didn't identify him. Doesn't know who it was. Knows hardly anyone here. Himself belongs to a different brigade altogether anyhow, attached here by mistake. Wants to get back to his own unit. Why've they stuck him here in the first place? He misses his pals, and besides, they're getting their discharge soon, and then where will he be? . . .

They remove him—

Little by little, in the massing darkness, understanding comes to my son. His face unfolds, his eyes clear, his figure straightens. He adjusts the rifle and comes to life. And I who feel my collapse imminent want to climb onto him.

"This morning, at school, the Head informs me," I speak to him at last, "it's been a mad day. . . ."

The ring around us tightens, the men cleave to us. The story of his death and resurrection thrills them. They press jokes upon the two of us, want to hear all the particulars. We both stand trembling, smiling weakly.

The officers start breaking it up, sending the men back to the half-tracks. The night deepens, the patrol ought to be on its way, there is still a war on.

And we are suddenly alone, both of us in helmets but myself unarmed, with only the torn flap on my heart.

"What's with you?" I whisper at him rapidly, with the last of my strength.

And only now he looks at me, stunned, that I have closed with him, come as far as this and by the very border hemmed him in.

"You can see for yourself . . ." he whispers with something of despair, with bitterness, as though it were I who issued call-up orders, "such a loss of time . . . so pointless . . ."

And how to give him some point, some meaning, but quickly, hurriedly, in the shadow of the vehicles which are starting up their engines again, before he disappears to the vague nightly lines of the desert, and before I myself should fall before him into a deep slumber.

Not dreaming yet, but asleep. I mean: my heart asleep. Nod on my feet, with weakness, with hunger, and diminish under a star-tossed sky and a moon rising in the east. Clouds start to move, the setting changes and consciousness fades. Little by little the senses are quenched as well. I do not hear the shots flaring up again in the distance, do not smell these rushes, the desert mallow; and what I hold in my hand drops soundlessly; it is from a blurring figure that I take leave, flutter my hand like a defeated actor to the beam of light cast at me from one of the half-tracks, and yield my body to someone willing to take it (someone different again, very young) and get me back onto some tank, shut the steel plate upon me. And once again beside a red bulb, without headlights, in the dark, I begin the journey back.

And it was then that I noticed for the first time that I had lost the text. Entire chapters. I would not have passed a single test, not the easiest of tests. The last verses were slipping and being ground by the creaking chains.

After this opened Job his mouth and cursed his day—
A prayer of Habakkuk the prophet upon Shigionoth—
A Psalm of David when in the wilderness of Judah—

In the year that king Uzziah died—
To the Musician upon Shoshannim—
The song of songs—
Hallelujah—

Not allowed to dream yet. By the light of a clouded moon, at the forward position, I discover a civilian car, headlights burning, engine humming softly, no one inside. Next they are taking, almost pushing me, toward one of their huge tents, and there, by the light of one pale bulb, between field radios, twisted telephone cables, and nude photographs stirring against the tent-flaps my daughter-in-law, standing between the beds, surrounded by signalers who are gazing enchanted at the young, windblown woman who has turned up at nightfall in their tent.

"He not killed," I tell her at once in my broken English, grimy, on the verge of dreams.

But she knows already, and all she wants now is to fall upon me, wild with excitement, having been certain all along it was nothing but a private delusion of mine.

But I forestall her, and insensibly, drowsily, through a thousand veils, I take two steps, getting entangled in cables, rubbing against the pinups, fall upon her, kiss her brow, stroke her hair, and a delicate smell of perfume steals into my first dream, the cool touch of her skin, smooth, lacking warmth.

This New Left—

Surreptitiously perfumed—

Seeking warmth—

And then she breaks down. The signalers are stunned. About to cry, but first she says something in rapid English, repeating it more slowly, unexpectedly casting about for Hebrew words as well, and at last crying, silently, making no sound.

And only now I become aware of an old signaler in a corner of the tent, bent over a field telephone, trying to find out, unhopefully, with someone very distant, the dead man's true identity.

And again someone comes to fetch me, leads me and her to a tent at the far end of the camp and offers us the rumpled beds of soldiers out on ambush, to sleep in till morning. Then they bring food in mess tins, a bottle with some leftover wine in honor of the Sabbath eve, light a candle on the floor, and leave us to ourselves, my daughter-in-law and me, in the translucent darkness of one quivering candle, in the close air of the Jordan Valley.

And I, crazed and exhausted with hunger, the smell of the food stupefies me. And thus, seated on the bed, the dishes on the floor at my feet, without looking at her, without strength left to speak English, I stoop and eat like a savage, crouching over the food, with a misshapen fork and without a knife, sleepily devouring the army food that tastes wonderful to me, mingled with the smells and flavors of gunpowder, saltpeter, desert dust, sweat;

set the bottle to my lips and gulp down cheap wine, sweet and tepid and reeking of rifle grease and tank fuel, and right away getting drunk, as though someone were striking me with dull inward remote blows that are growing sharper and sharper.

Shots. Human beings shooting at each other again. I wake up, find myself lying on the bed, the helmet that I had grown used to as to a skullcap taken off my head, my shoes removed. The moon is gone, the candle extinguished and the darkness grown deep. A new wind has set up, gently beating against the tent flaps, bringing in a current of cool desert air. Without lifting myself up, very heavy, my face sticky with food remnants like a baby's, I make out her profile; sitting up on the other bed, her long hair in wild confusion about her, a soldier's battle dress over her shoulders, her face open, feet bare, sitting and sucking upon a cigarette. Half the night gone and she still awake. Hasn't touched the food. Her head turned toward me, gazing at me in fascination, in wonder, and the dread that drove her through several barriers last night in order to reach this place deepens, as though by my power I had killed him, as though by my power brought him back to life, as though I had not wished but to indicate one possibility. . . .

The firing does not stop. Single shots, and it is as if they had changed direction. But I feel I am growing more and more used to them. She is not frightened either, does not stir, even though now he might really get killed, somewhere out there, on his half-track slowly grinding down a trail.

I must still go over the moment when I learned of his death.

Summer morning, the sky cut depthwise, June, last days, I rise late, stunned, as after an illness, straight into the sun.

The bells are ringing and I am swept slowly up the stairs upon the turmoil of students who suck me upward in their tide, into the corridors. Move along the open classroom doors, past weary teachers' faces, arrive at my Twelfth and find them quiet, aloof, long-haired, Bibles dropping to the floor. One of them is by the blackboard filling it with flowers, dozens of white crumbling flowers.

I mount the platform and they raise their eyes at me. The room is dim, curtains drawn. And I realize: I am not important to them any more, have lost my power over them, they have done with me, I already belong to the past.

How well I know that look; yet I never feared it, for I knew—they would come back in the end. In a few years I would find them about, with their wives or husbands, running after their babies with a faint stoop, and when I would meet them—self-conscious, holding shopping baskets—in the street, I would regain my power over them. If even for an instant, for a split second.

But these last years the parting becomes difficult. They are off to the deserts, far away; I mean, this supple flesh, the erect heads, the young eyes. And there are those who do not come back. Several class-years already. Some disappear. And some balance is upset with me. I remain troubled. This pain of theirs, the advantage of an experience in which I have no share. And even those who do come back, though they walk with their children and their shopping baskets, there is something veiled in their eyes, they stare at me blankly, almost ignore me, as though I had deceived them somewhere. I mean, as though with the material itself I had deceived them. As though everything we taught them—the laws, the proverbs, the prophecies—as though it had all collapsed for them out there, in the dust, the scorching fire, the lonely nights, had all failed the test of some other reality. But what other reality? Lord of Hosts, Lord God—*what* other reality for heaven's sake? Does anything really change? I mean, these imaginary signs of revolution.

And I am seized with unquiet, start handing out the test papers, pass between the rows myself and lay them on their desks. And the silence around me deepens. They read, give a little sigh, then pull out clean sheets of paper and start drafting their straightforward, efficient, unimaginative answers in the bald, arid style that may suddenly, unaccountably, take a lyrical turn, only to dry up again and expire in the desert.

They'll be the death of me—

And there is my son, returned from the United States, clumsy, hair grown, such a gentle professor, no longer so young. Has brought along a campus girl, a slender student, cloaked in a worn and tasseled garment, and on her shoulders, strapped into a sort of rucksack, a small, pale child who speaks only English. And they alight from the plane and look at me as though they had brought some new gospel, tidings of a revolution, of some other reality, wonderful and unknown. . . .

And I suddenly feel tears spring to my eyes. Still wandering between the desks, past Bibles on the floor, stoop and pick one up here and there. The students follow me with their eyes, already longing to crib, or at least pass on a whisper that they believe might help them, might add another fraction to their grades, even though they are abandoning it all soon, leaving empty classrooms behind them, a pile of chairs in a corner, a clean blackboard, traces of their names scored on desks as on tombstones.

And all of a sudden I long for a different parting, one that will be scored on their memories. In a whirl of emotion I cross to the windows and jerk the curtains aside, bespatter them with heavy splashes of sunlight as drops of blood. Go to the door and open it wide, stand on the threshold, half my face to the corridor and half to the class. And I know the suspense they are in. Am I setting them a trap? Am I here or am I not?

And then I see the Head from afar, striding sadly and pensively along the empty corridor. Approaches slowly, heavily, like an obsolete tank. Something deep has aged in him these past few years. In a year or so he too will have to retire. He lifts his head and sees me standing on the threshold, lowers it again as though I were a stone or spirit. He still assumes I do not want to talk to him. As though three years had not sufficed us. And in the room the whispering swells, and the swish of papers. Passing on the answers to each other. But I make no move. My face is turned to the corridor window, its display of summer bright and full. The Hills of Judea in the distance, the Hills of Moab, and all the rest. And the image of the students behind me is reflected in the window as well, fused upon the scenery, on a patch of blue, on the treetops, faraway aerials, the hum of aircraft.

And the Head stops beside me. For the first time in three years. Very pale. And must break the silence at once.

Five or six hours ago—
In the Jordan Valley—
Killed on the spot—

Missile Base 612

1

And in the night he knows a brief spell of pre-dawn wakefulness, as though someone had pushed him off the mattress to the rug, seized him by the collar and plucked him off the floor, dumped him in a chair to face the gray TV screen gleaming in the dark, where now a vague reflection of his face begins to shimmer. And sleep-worn but wide awake, he sticks a bitter pipe between his teeth, wants to say something, would even hold a little lecture.

Some minutes pass and he starts prowling about the

dark flat, wanders in and out of the kitchen, the lav, the child's room; opens the bedroom door and stands in the doorway, casting a shadow over his wife's body which lies aslant the twin bed. He lingers, waiting to hear if she will mumble something in her sleep, moan perhaps, then retreats, turns back to the living room, goes to the radio and fumbles between low distant music, readings from the Koran, and faraway signals; drops into an armchair and broods on the impending divorce and how he'll have to take the whole place apart, and presently his strength fails him, his breathing grows harsh, he kneels on the rug, tugs at the sheet, smells people's footmarks, and falls into a deep sleep again.

In the morning when the light floods in through the large balcony door, nothing is left of all his early awakening except a red bulb in the radio which has got stuck between two stations.

And then he gets up, puts the kettle on, washes, dresses, folds the mattress, sheets, blanket, removes the traces of the night and goes to wake the kid. These past weeks he has been lifting him out of bed as he is, carried him still half asleep into the kitchen, put him on a chair and talked at the drowsy child while he sips his coffee.

He hasn't exchanged a word with his wife for months. The first shots were fired long ago, the cause obscured; now it's open war. Once they could squabble a whole day long, not letting go of each other, even forgetting to go to work sometimes; and till deep into the night, in hot fury, occasionally smashing a piece of crockery coming to hand. Now it's each to himself. Urgent messages are passed through the child, who has grown older lately, graver, whom the new silence in the house is grinding down.

Each of them cooks for himself, and they take turns to eat. On the stairs, at chance encounters, they stiffen for a moment, bow their heads—the gestures of stubborn knights. If she would die, he sometimes thinks, late in the evening and she not home yet from one of her unaccountable night journeys, he laying out the mattress for another solitary night in the living room, waiting in vain for the sound of key in front door, falling asleep in a rage and waking before dawn to find her in her bed, sleeping peacefully, slantwise, unstirring. And in the morning he is alone, dressing his son, giving him breakfast, taking him to school, driving to the university, looking for hitchhikers to draw into conversation. But it's the spring vacation now and there are no students at this time of morning, and when he gets stuck in a line of cars at an intersection, two cleaning women from the university spot him, make a dash for the crawling car, and he stops, lets them in, not acknowledging their thanks, and fiercely, almost savagely, he gallops off with them through this freakish spring—a drab spring blowing with dank breezes, hangover of a winter that hasn't been much of a winter either but cold clear skies and sickly buds shriveling on their branches.

He crosses the university campus slowly, deliberately, looking for someone to accost; arrives at the nearly empty library, spreads his papers over a desk by the window, goes to take out Aristotle's *Metaphysics* from the reserved section, and in utter silence, with unutterable slowness, not concentrating, he starts to read the ancient, difficult text which he will have to explain to his students next year, his eyes continually straying from the lines to the gray world beyond the window. This sabbatical is also crumbling fast, a year without students, adrift in the library. It's been three years since he published anything. His friends say he's finished, dead. He ought to have tackled something long ago. And again he jumps up to look for someone, anyone, to flip newspaper pages in another room, wander through corridors, return to his desk, read another page or two before he is up and out again, walking in a cloud of tobacco smoke to the bursary to see if they've calculated his salary correctly, from there to his mailbox to find only a slender volume of poetry sent him by an old schoolmate who each year, come spring, publishes at his own expense a batch of wishy-washy love poems. He tears off the wrapper, glances at the inscription, turns a few pages and is filled with weariness. Then back to the corridors to resume his aimless rambling, to follow a slight, delicate girl student, stop with her to study the notice board, holding his breath, watching her furtively, it's been a long time, he's ready to fall in love, desperately, at a hint. Eventually he retreats; back to the reading room, to his book, listlessly, with growing reluctance, to discover after twenty pages that he hasn't taken in anything; and he starts anew, forces himself to summarize each passage like a first-year student. His gaze fixes itself on some grains of sand beating against the window; a few miraculously gain entrance, land by his plodding pen.

Toward noon he returns the book to the reserved section.

"Shall I keep it for this afternoon?" asks the elderly woman librarian, already used to seeing him show up suddenly toward nightfall.

"No, I'm flying to Sinai this afternoon to lecture at a missile base," he informs her casually, with a smile, hoping to rise in her esteem.

"So for when?"

"Tomorrow morning, as usual."

She does not even look up.

"Yes, I'll be back tonight. . . ." he prods her gently.

But the woman just gives him an absent smile, hasn't listened very closely, or perhaps it doesn't strike her as anything particularly wonderful, these shortened distances.

Yet he himself had been amazed when a girl from the Army's lecturers pool rang up a week ago to inform him of this lecture. Be at the airport at three, they'll fly you back after, she had told him. As far as I'm concerned, he had said, I don't mind staying the night. But she insisted: No, they'll fly you back. But I wouldn't mind staying once I've come that far. She had refused to give in, though, as if in all that desert there really was no place for him. Ah well, how could she have known that at home he sleeps on a mattress in the living room?

2

He had been transferred to this unit of itinerant lecturers early in the winter. Before that they used to call him up twice a year, summer and winter, for a fortnight of guarding two huge electrical transmission towers planted in the middle of some field. The long nights of guard duty had been a growing ordeal, the hours dragging out endlessly till at last, around midnight, time would stop completely. And in a trance of fatigue, his mind vacant, his rifle tossed into the corn, he would slip through the crisscross of iron bars, sit down inside the tower like a caged ape, listen to the monotonous hum of electric current overhead, and wait helplessly for the frozen sky to start moving again.

One morning a young lecturer on reserve duty had given them a talk about official Israeli policy. After the lecture—which he had considered rather crude—he had made inquiries about the lecturers pool and the qualifications needed to join it. Eventually he had gone there, introduced himself complete with academic degree and a tentative list of subjects, and had been accepted at once, to his own surprise. Now he would be called on to give a lecture once every week or two, wandering between various outfits, training camps, strongholds, remote spots he never knew existed. And the country spreads itself before him as he goes on his wanderings, skipping up hill and down dale and speaking, preaching to soldiers.

And all at once—a different audience; no longer a dozen philosophy students with metaphysical texts in front of them, fencing with him, waging stiff battles over every word, but motley crowds, boys and men who assemble on command and are placed in front of him, his words wafting over them as a gentle breeze. And he is treated with respect, is offered coffee or soft drinks, invited to meals, and when he displays an interest they show him their new weapons too—a bridge-laying tank or a bent-barrel gun. Sometimes, when he happens to arrive at some front-line position in the afternoon and his listeners must be routed out of bed first, he mounts the observation posts on his own initiative, to peer through giant binoculars at the other side, watch the tiny enemy popping up here and there in the dunes, filling sandbags at leisure.

And he speaks. In field, outpost, mess hall; under a blue sky, under a canvas roof, on the top of a hill or in a bunker underground; early in the morning, at noon, and after supper; repeats the same two or three lectures over and over again, jokes and all. The ease with which the words spout from his mouth surprises even him. He does still preserve a tiny quiver of anticipation, every time anew, but it ebbs swiftly after the first few words. And the soldiers' faces before him—a many-colored multitude. Dozing, yawning, tense, laughing, irritated. And he always still relishes the thought that presently he'll wind up his lecture, answer last questions and be free to leave them, and it's they who'll be left to the long night of guard duty. In vain he tries to keep a face or two of his ever-changing audience in mind. The landscape, on the other hand, does stay with him—the view of a distant hill, a dry river bed, a mudtrack hugging a security fence. And the weapons too. The tanks, the swivel guns, the infra-red sights of machine guns. And nowadays, missiles as well. He hasn't seen the missiles yet.

3

He leaves the university at midday, and the sky is a gray whirlpool. Mercilessly he cuts through the small flock of girls waiting for a lift, races homeward. All at once it strikes him again as something marvelous that he's going to be in Sinai this very day, and back tonight.

Arriving, he delves into the mailbox downstairs as if in breathless expectation of long-awaited, unknown tidings; inspects his wife's letters and returns them to the box; runs quickly over his own unimportant stuff and tears it up as he climbs the stairs. He enters the silent flat, makes straight for the kitchen, warms up the food he's prepared for himself earlier in the week, its charred flavor getting nastier every day. Then he clears the table, washes up, enters the bedroom to collect his army gear and is startled to find her still asleep in the half-light, at the same nocturnal slant across the bed, her expression peaceful as though time had stood still. What's happened? He feels a fleeting urge to wake her, to ask, but what's it to him, after all. If she were dead and done with, but her deep breaths ripple through the room. A glass of water stands at the bedside and sleeping pills show up white in the darkness. He collects his army clothes—khaki pants, old leather jacket, gray shirt, high boots; undresses, moves around a little in his underwear, makes some noise, but she doesn't move, her uncovered feet pale marble. Briefly, absently, desire stirs. But the sun piercing the clouds kindles cracks between the lowered blinds, casts arrows of light at him. He raises the blinds partly to see the sky swept clear, glances at the quiet street, at the children returning from school. He waits awhile, and then his son appears around the corner too, alone, trudging uphill, weighed down by the heavy satchel. And with a surge of love for him he lowers the blind softly, puts on his clothes, sticks an old hat on his head, takes his army bag, and rushes out.

He meets the child downstairs, flushed, worn out by his schoolday, bruised here and there with the fights he's been getting into lately. He pulls him close, smooths his hair, adjusts disheveled clothing and showers instructions upon him. What to eat, what to do, what to tell his mother if she asks about him. He has flown to Sinai to lecture at a missile base and he'll be back tonight. The kid doesn't take in either the flight or Sinai, only the missiles. A smile lights up in his eyes. Real missiles? You bet. But don't wake her up. If anyone phones tell them Daddy's out, Mummy's asleep. That's all. The kid listens, keeps nodding his head, saying yes, all right, all right, already looking forlorn. And now the lecturer takes him in his arms, kisses him, and the boy stands still, lowers his head, odd how he freezes these days, blushes even, when kissed by his father. And now the sky clouds over again too, and a few drops fall and cease at once, as if by way of experiment, and he hurries to his car, on his way to the airport.

4

He watches Tel Aviv tilt slowly sideways, seesawing, as though straining to turn over, then clouds dropping swiftly on top of it, and then it starts to sink, is covered by the sea; gray-green, turbulent sea, nipped by winds, whipped to feathery crests. Now it's all sea as far as the skyline. And what is left of the sky? A welter of murky light. A dubious spring.

He opens his old student-case-turned-army-bag and inspects its contents. The poetry volume he has received this morning and stuffed in here at the last moment, headache pills, sleeping pills, pep pills, tobacco pouch, a rotting apple from his previous lecture, razor blades, and finally the pages of his lecture in a crushed roll, notes written in outsize script. "Zionism in Confrontation with Other Ideologies," "The Israeli as Jew," "The Face of Israeli Society under Drawn-out Struggle." He invariably picks his subject at the last moment, going by his mood, by the noise around him, the quality of the light on the upturned faces before him, the distance home. Sometimes he comes, talks fluently for an hour without interruption, and departs as soon as he's finished. At other times he stirs up a discussion, trumps up imaginary problems, and starts arguing with stubborn composure.

And meanwhile the plane keeps steadily on its western course, the engines at full power, the coastline long vanished, as though they were heading for Europe, not for the desert. Yet before long it will veer, start the broad curve backward, inland.

He is the only civilian aboard. The soldiers have removed their caps, shoved their weapons under the upholstered seats, settled down to rustle newspapers, solve crossword puzzles, converse in low voices. The girl sitting next to him, a small, delicate girl-soldier, huddles against the window with her evening paper, as if afraid he'll touch her, though he has not meant to touch her, just wants to talk a little, exchange a few words, without hope, without expectations. He is still unsure of his liberty. His relations with women are clumsy. He gives up in advance.

Over her head he watches the slow return of the land avidly. Dunes, houses, fields, last orchards strung out over sallow hills. The sky is clear, and the sun which had been hidden all morning is there, sailing ahead of them in its full glory. The throb of the engines and the dry, summery heat are sleep-inducing, and all around him heads drop, eyes glaze over druggedly. He tries to sleep a little himself but is still too eager, his eyes searching the slow-moving desert landscape below him for novelties. The pipe is heavy in his hand. Gently he catches the evening paper slipping at him from the other seat, then the feather-light body of the girl-soldier who seems to have relaxed her guard, leaning against him drowsily as the plane dips; a hairpin drops into his lap, softly his lust awakens, and all of a sudden he conceives a provocative, subversive lecture —at a missile base of all places, before the pick of the Army.

And now they are deep into the desert, the soldiers are coming to life, the girl beside him pulls away too, opens her eyes and blinks away a tear. He holds out the paper and she smiles vacantly, touching her hair which has come loose.

"When are we going to get there?" he asks, handing back the hairpin as well.

She throws a swift glance at the aimless, amorphous mass of desert:

"We're there already. . . ."

It's true. The roar of the engines is falling off, the plane has begun to lose altitude, and as they hover about the runway he still sees nothing but wasteland, his eyes on the window drinking in every detail, thrilled to discover the row of bright hook-nosed fighter-bombers.

"Phantoms . . ." he identifies them with that curious excitement that all weapons rouse in him these days.

"Just painted dummies . . ." The delicate girl-soldier smiles, stares at him as though only now really noticing him. "Have you never been here before?"

"Well, yes, in '56 . . . just for a few hours . . . somewhere around here . . ."

"In '56?" she repeats, puzzled. "What happened in '56?"

"The Sinai campaign. I was dropped here by parachute, on one of these hills."

The plane comes to a stop and there is a general bustle of rising, donning caps, slinging up guns, crowding to the exit. A stewardess, who has kept herself well out of sight during the trip, stands by the door dressed in a colorful uniform, bestows a personal smile on each passenger, bids them good-by as though they were vacationers arrived at a holiday-camp. He inches forward behind the girl-soldier, his eyes on the nape of her neck, but once on the field he loses her, as usual, without even a parting word.

5

A desert airfield, people milling about, a kind of Wild West. Dozens of vehicles by the fence like a line of hackney coaches waiting for fare. Station wagons, jeeps, vans, lorries, half-tracks, even an old tank sent especially to pick up two soldiers.

Tired, needled by a thin headache, his dead pipe bitter in his mouth, he wanders about the emptying field, the old briefcase in one hand and in the other the reels of motion picture he's been given at the airport to pass on to the local education officer. It is the picture in a thin black suitcase which attracts the notice of a dark, skinny soldier to him. He approaches at a slouch, carrying a bulky transistor radio held together by string, and intoning an Egyptian hit parade in a shaky whine. He holds out a scrap of paper with the lecturer's name slightly misspelled in a soft, feminine handwriting.

"Yes, that's me. . . ."

The soldier crumples the note and drops it as though relieved of a heavy burden, leads the way to a big empty truck, and with the transistor on the seat between them pouring out its tunes, they drive slowly across a large bustling camp.

And already he is questioning the driver.

"Going straight to the battery?"

"No, only as far as command."

"And where's the battery?"

"Not far . . ."

"Figure I'll make it back tonight?"

"Sure."

"And who're the men there?"

"Regulars."

"All high school graduates?"

"Not all. . . . What you lecturing about?"

"Oh, I don't know . . . I'll make up my mind when I get there . . . maybe I'll let the men choose. . . ."

He always prefers not to reveal his subjects in advance. They appear old-fogyish at first sight, heavy, off-putting. . . .

"Give 'em a talk on drugs," the driver suggests magnanimously. "Know about drugs?"

"Drugs?" says the lecturer, faintly amused.

"Yeah. Couple of weeks back I brought them a lecturer on drugs. . . . Guys loved it. . . ."

"So what do you want another lecture for?"

"Why not . . . it's interesting . . . like maybe about other kinds of drugs. . . ."

The lecturer smiles to himself, a trickle of sweet smoke escaping his lips.

"Do the men take drugs?"

"Bet they'd like to. . . ."

And all around a land of great drought, hills and copper mounds and army garbage, shacks, structures, and vehicles driving about, to the left and right of them, crossing in front, overtaking every which way. And from time to time they are made to stop at a rope barrier, one end held by a dark-skinned fellow, the driver's counterpart, lolling in a frayed wicker chair, a soldier twisted and paralyzed with idleness.

"Where you going?"

"Lemme through."

"Where you going?"

"None of your bloody business. Lemme through. . . ."

"Where you going?"

"To 612. So lemme through, dammit. . . ."

But the other makes no move, sprawls full length, a wicked little grin on his face.

"What you got there?"

"None of your business. Lemme through."

"What you got there?"

"Lecturer."

And the rope drops before them.

6

And the truck rolls on, reaches a small service base, turns around a square, and pulls up beside a piece of sculpture hatched by an unequivocal military mind. The torn, rust-eaten tail of an Egyptian aircraft whose dim, slightly furry cracks gape at the missile which smashed into it and which has been resurrected here now, painted gaily and inscribed with biblical verses torn out of context.

"This is where I'm to drop you. . . ." The driver bangs the radio to silence it and flits away, drawn like a butterfly to a bunch of soldiers kicking at a ball in a far corner of the camp. Ah well, he is used to being transferred like this, handed on from one person to the other, one car to the next, sometimes left in a dim barracks, a communication trench, a storeroom, to wait till his listeners are rounded up for him.

He alights from the truck, strolls about the grounds, still with briefcase in one hand and film in the other; wanders between two rows of reddish prefabs, in the glaring light, stark summer light from an azure sky; inspects his surroundings as one who doesn't belong to this desert, this dull expanse of low, shapeless hills, the incoherent mixture of a great dead hush and camp noises—the roar of tanks, shouts, and wind-blown commands.

He takes a turn around the sculpture, taps the missile lightly and hears the echoing hollowness, peels a strip of metal from the shattered tail and is amazed at the ease with which the aircraft crumbles up between his fingers. Fifteen minutes pass and he is still alone. No one is coming for him. He approaches the playing soldiers, watches the brown bodies shiny with sweat pursue the ball in silence, in seeming fury. By now he can no longer even pick out his driver, who has doffed his shirt too and joined the game. He stands there puffing at his pipe and presently there is a faint stirring on the barren ground between his feet, a thin flurry of sand starts up as though a storm were about to arise from the earth. And as always in moments of waiting he already bemoans the time lost, confident that if he were seated in the library now he would be able to concentrate. The outline of the hills sharpens slightly. No one comes. They have forgotten him. Though why should he care, he is going back tonight whatever happens, they'll simply have to get him out of here. Still, he *would* like to deliver his lecture, feels a desire to speak, to speak without interruption, break a silence of several days. He returns to the truck, sounds a few brief blasts on the horn, walks over to one of the barracks, starts knocking at doors, one door, another, a third, and finds himself face to face with a gray, elderly colonel who appears to have surrounded himself with missiles: models of missiles glowing in the afternoon light, diagrams of missiles on the wall, photographs of them in action. An ideology of missiles.

The man hasn't noticed his hesitant entry, sits bent over a manual, absorbed in his reading.

"Excuse me . . ." holding out the call-up order.

The colonel looks up, removes his glasses, reaches for the order with smooth, almost effeminate hands, barely glances at it.

"No, that's not here . . . you want Ginger. . . ."

"Ginger?"

"The education officer . . . Lecturers are her domain. . . ."

And he points at the barracks across the road, hands back the order.

The lecturer retreats slowly, looking at the little missiles set out like toys on the shelves, longs to touch them, does touch them with his fingertips.

The colonel watches him curiously.

"What do you lecture about?"

And he flounders on the doorstep, sticks his pipe in his mouth, chews the stem, removes it. Well, he hasn't quite made up his mind yet—as though anyone cared, as though there were some intrinsic flaw about his subjects—well, let's say, something about Jewish identity, or some brief outline of Israeli society under drawn-out struggle. Or maybe, for instance, Zionism in confrontation with other ideologies, with the New Left for example. Depends on the audience. He won't mind just letting them ask him questions, anything that may occur to them, and he'll do his best to answer.

The officer appears somewhat taken aback, as though these subjects of his were rather peculiar, as though there were something original or faintly shocking about them to give him some ground for concern.

"Do you still want to get back tonight too?" he asks.

"They promised I would. . . ." He is seized by a sudden fear they mean to detain him. "The last plane . . . Do you think I won't make it?"

"You will."

And now he's in a hurry, shuts the door behind him, crosses the grounds, stops at a door, knocks, pushes it open, enters a darkened, chaotic room, something between office and girl's sanctum, and discovers by the light from the door, in the faint musty smell, a bed and a tangle of fiery red hair. A girl, a giant of a girl, a great redhead lying on her stomach under a blanket. Her clothes are all over the place, shirt and blue skirt, underwear in a heap beside a military phone. Filthy coffee cups, an empty wine bottle, a carpet of sunflower-seed shells on the floor.

Wearily he touches her. He could have lifted the bankket and lain down silently by her side till this evening ended and the hour of his departure came, but he only touches her, lightly, embittered.

"You Ginger?" he asks his own reflection looking at him out of two large blue eyes open on his face, and hands her the crumpled call-up order. "I'm the lecturer. I'm due at 612."

He already says "612" as if it were a familiar place, as if he'd moved among the batteries here for years.

She smiles, takes the order, stuffs it under her pillow unread.

"So you've arrived. . . ."

"I arrived half an hour ago. I've just been hanging around here, and I've got to get back tonight. We'll never make it this way."

"We will."

Again she smiles at him, a wide provocative grin, still under her blanket, naked no doubt. He smiles back, embarrassed, unnerved by his own smile. Such a giantess. Even if he had the time she'd be impossible for him. Stuck there in the silence he waits for her to emerge out of her blanket.

But she lies there still, her eyes laughing.

"We will, if you'll let me get dressed."

The blood rushes to his face as he turns to leave the dim room, the carpet of shells whispering underfoot. He leaves the door open, goes to the square, paces up and down beside the sculpture, very excited; and sees the flash and dazzle of white springing up there in the darkness he has left behind. She continues dressing at her leisure while he is already on his way back to her, not taking his eyes off, boldly, openly. And when she appears in the doorway, in a childish, much too short skirt, in sandals, zipping up a wind-cheater with faded captain's insignia, he is already there beside her, eyes raised to her face:

"Mind if I just make a phone call?"

"Homesick already?"

"No . . . something . . . it's just . . . I only . . ."

She puts him on her still-warm bed, gets him a line, and goes out. And at home the child picks up the receiver, and is joined by all the roar of the desert.

"Yoram, it's Daddy," he shouts into the trembling, breathing line.

But the boy fails to recognize the distorted voice.

"Daddy's away, Mummy's asleep," he hears the steady, disciplined voice through the turmoil.

"This is Daddy . . . can't you hear me?" he cries desperately.

But the child is gone and the roaring desert is gone with him and the line goes dead, and someone in the middle of another conversation, very near, apparently, lisps soft cajoling words of love at him.

And the redhead in the doorway, a pillar of fire, stands calmly observing his struggles with the phone.

"Finished?"

7

Actually he ought to go home at once, to the child wandering about there by itself, ought to shake the sleeping woman who must be out of her mind. Instead of which, he climbs into the battered, dirty jeep driven up by the girl, its floor strewn with yet more sunflower shells, mingling with machine-gun bullets, food tins whose wrapping has come off, gummy sweets sticking to military documents, a huge white brassiere between cans of lubricant. A mixture of war apparatus and feminine paraphernalia. And only now, sitting close to her, bending to put the briefcase and film between his feet, does he notice that she isn't so young any more; the slightly bowed shoulders, the resignation to her oversize self. Maybe she signed on as a regular, imagining that here, in this reddish desert, she'd be less conspicuous. His glance travels coolly over the large thighs, the pale flesh not taking a tan, yet affecting. What's growing here? This young generation, he thinks, amazed and faintly repulsed, his eyes on her enormous feet against the pedals. She waits for his eyes to complete their inspection and then smiles at him, sadly, as if all too familiar with herself; lifts a hand to smooth her hair, glowing crown of thorns, then starts the jeep savagely.

But drives slowly, as though sleepy still, circles the sculpture twice as though lost in thought, then turns onto a potholed road that lies straight as an arrow in front of them. And beyond the dusty windscreen lies the dreary desert, low, bleak hills, sand dunes; a stale, vapid landscape with its stubborn bushes growing under a layer of dust. This wearisome, war-worn desert, good for nothing except strategical vantage—even the approaching twilight hour cannot soften it.

"This landscape . . . so depressing . . ." he says, to break the silence, to make contact. For a moment she appears not to have heard, but then the jeep comes to a stop, in the middle of the empty road. She eyes him quizzically.

"You find the landscape depressing?"

This sudden braking, the direct question, as if it were a personal matter—his, or hers; as if there were any particular significance to what he says.

"Why does it depress you?"

He smiles, taken aback, the sun full in his face. They are alone in the sun, in space, all the army camps have long vanished behind them, and only the slow whirring of the engine accompanies the stuttered words he forces out in explanation. She listens tensely, her glance shifting from him to the scenery and back, as if anything could be done about it, as if the scenery were open to change or amendment.

"I suppose I've got used to it," she says apologetically. "I find it beautiful. . . ."

And then softly, with absurd politeness:

"I'm sorry. . . ."

"It's not your fault. . . ." He laughs, shrinks in his seat, graceless, knowing himself graceless. In his embarrassment he discovers a whole sunflower seed among the debris of shells, picks it up, cracks it, chews absently, waits to be in motion again, and slowly they drive on, still in second gear, crawling along the rough road as though they had all the time in the world, and it is nearly six, and he still has a lecture to give and get home again.

Another silence, and she still smiling at him, as though she wanted something from him, this titanic redhead bent over the wheel, her hair brushing the canvas roof flapping in the wind, while he stares at the hills around him, avoiding her eyes. A distant memory flickers through his mind.

"Have you never been here before?"

"Yes I have . . ." he replies quickly.

And once again the jeep stops, as if she couldn't talk while driving, as if his words called for careful study, at a standstill.

"I was here in '56."

"When?"

"In the Sinai campaign."

"Lecturing too?"

"No, of course not!" He grins—the idea! "I was dropped somewhere around here, on one of these hills. Maybe even that one there . . ." pointing at a hill on the near skyline which is slowly turning crimson.

She listens thoughtfully, her hands in her lap. He is never going to give that lecture.

"Every lecturer who comes here goes on about some battle or other he took part in. . . . Once we had one—told stories, talked my head off, in the end it turned out he was talking about the First World War."

"The *Second* . . ." he corrects her.

"The *First,*" she insists. "Me too, I thought he must mean the Second World War. He didn't seem that old. . . ."

He doesn't answer, looks away, beginning to lose his patience. The girl's muddleheaded.

"I didn't hurt your feelings, did I?"

Her voice, very gentle.

"No." Startled, he looks at her sitting beside him, hands loose in her lap, smiling sweetly at him. And with a jolt the jeep starts again and the pipe slips from his hand, drops to the floor, rolls under the pedals. He bends but she forestalls him, picks it up, but instead of placing it in his outstretched hand she thrusts it between his lips in an intimate gesture, and he smells her, covertly, the smell of a big queer animal. So that's her game, is it?

And now he is faintly excited. And they drive on in silence at the same slow, nerve-racking pace, approach the crimson hills, and he's afraid to say a word or she'll stop again and this journey will never end, while by now he is bent on giving this lecture, passionately, an ache in his chest. The twilight, the lengthening shadows, the emptiness around. In this desert, this Sinai—this is where he wants to speak. Where are they? The people, the nation. To stand before them, hear the buzz, the murmuring, the creaking of chairs or stones. Briskly to pull the sweater over his head, fling it over a chair or on the ground, remove his wristwatch, place the notes in front of him, and start speaking as a first caress, in a sweet voice soon to harden. To envelop them, penetrate the veil of lethargy and seep through their attention, drive in the words at an ever-quickening rhythm, and see them surrender, eyes shining, mouth opening in surprise, in resistance, then in a smile of pleasure. Till he is quite becalmed, starts retreating, drawing himself out of them, lightly smooth over final questions, dab at the sweat, leave a few question marks, a few vague promises for the future, smile self-consciously, gather up the notes, the watch, pull on the sweater, and get out.

The jeep picks up speed with a humming of air through the wheels. He looks at the approaching hills, first clouds looming in the distance.

"Is the Canal visible from here?" he asks unthinkingly, half to himself, and at once regrets the question. But she hasn't heard, or at any rate doesn't stop but drives on, only turns the wheel a bit, leaves the road, sweeps onto a dirt track and without slowing down, without shifting gear, in one rush, starts climbing a hill, at an ever steeper angle, regardless of any track, straight up as if aiming for the sky. Flintstones catapult from the plunging wheels. A bare waste all around, no sign of a house, a missile, a man.

"This it?" Wearily he climbs out of the jeep, looks for the missiles, but he's already used to finding his listeners hidden behind ridges and down dry river beds.

"Not yet. You wanted to see the Canal."

"Oh, never mind, thanks, it's getting late," and he turns back to the jeep.

"Come here . . ."

Calls him like a dog.

And the sense of freedom gripping him suddenly—

8

An unexpectedly strong wind is blowing here. He holds onto his hat, bows his head, but the wind tugs at him, winds come from every side and pounce on him as though they had lain in wait. Ten past six already. The sky has darkened, the light grown murky. The last plane back is at nine. She'll have to see that he gets there, this redhead. First he's had to wake her up and now she chooses to go gallivanting about the hills with him. She's taken a fancy to him, apparently. He follows her over the rocky hillside polished by the winds to a pale, sickly pink. Great big strides she takes, bobbing up and down, hunched with long habit of minimizing her tall stature. Her hair blazes in front of him. But a few hours ago he was still sitting in the university reading room, a feeble, woolgathering intellectual; and now here he is—far from human habitation, hundreds of miles to the south, on a hill of stone, clambering after this pillar of fire who does as she pleases. What does she want of him? Could she want him to make love to her in the short time left to his lecture? Perhaps other lecturers before him had made love to her here. He shivers, his eyes on her strong feet, sapphire flashing white over rock.

They reach the top in a few minutes. It isn't a very high hill, there are higher ones around, but it looks out straight at a gap in the mountain-ridge ahead and a wide horizon beyond. Breathlessly he catches up with her, and she points out the Canal to him, far away to the west. A brief, alarming glitter of blue. The sun is going down over the coasts of Egypt. And distant objects—rocks, hillocks, bushes—seem to float in the air by a trick of the falling light. She is standing very close to him, a full head taller, his hair grazing her captain's bars. Her freckled face smiles at him again.

"Still depressed by the landscape?" As to a small child she speaks to him.

"Less so. . . ." He laughs, knocks out his pipe hard against a stone. Could he touch her? He steps up on a low rock to poise himself over her, suddenly thinks of his wife and son.

"Maybe it's here they dropped you?"

Maybe.

A brief silence.

"What're you going to lecture about?"

"If we ever get there, you mean?" he asks, irony in his voice, and resignation.

"Why shouldn't we?"

And once again he flounders through his catalogue of subjects. His eyes on the ground, he starts listing the various possibilities in a low voice. The face of society in drawn-out struggle, or—The Israeli's Jewishness, or even—Zionism in confrontation with other ideologies. To provoke a discussion or something. Occasionally they just ask questions, anything that comes into their mind, and he answers.

She hears him out evenly, her eyes on the setting sun, as though his words didn't touch her, as though they swerved and fell on the rocks about her. He grins, stoops to pluck a leaf from a scorched, dusty balsam bush at his feet, notices a scrap of torn fabric, and farther down a couple of rusted, wind-worn jerry cans, the loose chain of a tank, a soot-blackened square of canvas, empty food tins, smashed munition crates—the relics of a vanquished army camp coming to light on the stony soil as on a strip of exposed ocean floor.

"Have they heard all that stuff before?" he asks with a surge of unreasonable despair.

She climbs up on a rock, looks down kindly at him, acts as though she still had all the time she might want, and all of a sudden he feels as though an eternity had passed since he came here, and he looks at the horizon and a sense of peace comes over him as well. Forget about the lecture and touch her, just touch her and the words will come later. And promptly he is gripped by excitement, stoops over the bush again to break off a sprig, to smell, to chew something, rouse himself, and then he notices that the bush at his feet isn't a bush at all but a heap of half-buried old clothes growing out of the earth. A crumbling tunic, a riddled, rust-eaten water canteen attached to an outworn military belt, a pair of mildewed trousers. He kicks at them lightly and starts, flinches, looks again, appalled. These are the remains of a human body, how come he didn't notice before? An ancient Egyptian soldier hidden in the sand, a hastily buried corpse, pale gray bones marking out a vanished form.

He looks up at her, and she, casually:

"That used to be the lecturer on Zionism . . . didn't hit it off with the men . . . annoyed them . . ."

Vainly he scans her face for a smile. Still grave, she points at the tumble of canvas and smashed crates:

"And that's the lecturer on Israeli society. Failed to convince them. Too sanguine . . ."

And now he laughs—a brief, muffled snort. He glances about him, leans toward her, searches her face for the smile, but she remains grave, only her eyes twinkle. Not muddleheaded after all then. He is drawn to her, points to a large smudge in the dark wadi.

"And who's that?"—teasingly.

"That one preached Jewish ethics," she flashes back at once, "put everybody to sleep, including himself, and when he woke up . . ."

She stops, falls silent.

The lecturer puffs at his pipe, and the smoke twirls blue in the light dying on their clothes. He hugs his briefcase closer to him, already grown restless, shivery. A star lights up in the sky and all of a sudden he loses confidence.

"Funny sort of lecturers . . ." he says, trying to keep up the note of banter—here on this barren hill exposed to the vast landscape, to the distant strip of water in the west still glowing with daylight . . . "dressed in those old ragged greatcoats . . ."

At last she smiles.

"Yes, that's how they always come here, dressed in their oldest clothes. They figure they're being sent to the back of beyond. Show up to lecture in high boots, old briefcases, funny hats. . . ."

He touches his own, reddens.

"Yes . . . hat is a bit funny. . . ."

Now he'll take her. Just a little courage. To hold her, suppress the slight nausea and seek the smooth tender place in her flesh, draw her mouth to him for a first kiss. He isn't going to get to that missile base tonight anyway.

He takes his hat off, throws it down, approaches her, but she slips away, starts downhill to the jeep, now a blurred mass in the fast-falling darkness. She bends down beside one of the wheels, picks something up. Stone? Skull?

"And this one imagined he could answer any question. . . ."

And laughing wildly she gets in, starts.

9

And the missile base turns out to have been only a short distance away all along, on a hill dug up as an antheap, well camouflaged, none of it visible except a pinpoint of light floating high on top of a tall aerial. But as soon as they halt at the gate in the gray dust he hears the rumble —as if the entire antheap were throbbing. And beyond the barrier he sees the slowly rotating radar scanners, the huge camouflage nets, and blank, egg-shaped domes from within which one can eavesdrop on the depths of space. And meanwhile the redhead is already scolding the guards for dawdling—impatiently, loftily, as if they were to blame for her wasted time. And then they are driving uphill again furiously, raising a cloud of dust, and the throbbing around them increases, large dug-in generators producing a din and a great blast of air.

And all of it lightless, not a glimmer of light. All the lights are hidden and buried. And here finally are the missile pits, real missiles, not quite as big as he'd imagined. And the girl maneuvers along twisting roads, always aiming upward. And now metal screens flow on both sides of them as the jeep gathers momentum, and metal-roofed communication trenches, metal steps dropping down into the earth, and gradually the ground itself becomes plated in iron. They draw up just below the crest of the hill, next to an enormous, thundering generator, and she leaps out nimbly, opens some door, is sucked in by a great spill of light, leaves him standing outside, briefcase in one hand, suitcase with film in other; and after a few seconds she pops out again, comes and shouts something at him over the fearful racket, but he doesn't catch a word, smiles in utter confusion, draws nearer to her. In the end she leans over him and wrenches the suitcase from his tight grip, takes it away. The OC has gone off somewhere and she's going to look for him. She opens the door again and ushers him into the brilliance now, and all at once the night seems dispelled and he finds himself in the middle of a bright noonday.

10

It is the blue camouflage paint on the windows and the yellow light of bare bulbs reflected in them that has created the momentary illusion of deep, spring-sky noon.

But then it turns out to be nothing but a military office after all, or maybe Operations itself, for the walls are covered with maps and charts. Two sergeants are playing chess, the board on a camp bed between them. They glance up wordlessly as he enters, then look away again, exchange a brief smile but say nothing. Ah well, he is familiar with the slight numbness, the curious embarrassment that comes over soldiers when suddenly confronted with a lecturer. He puts his briefcase on the floor among a litter of old magazines and tattered thrillers, and sinks into a plush Egyptian armchair, piece of loot from one or another war.

Silence. Only the dull roar of the generator outside.

Crushed by the silence again he rises, starts fidgeting about the room, inspecting the roster, the missile setup, charts marked with black circles and computer codes for every hill and mountain. Arrows point straight at the heart of Egypt, at the Nile meandering on its way into the depths of Sudan.

Now the two men are watching him.

"Won't you sit down. . . ."

"That's all right . . . thanks . . ."—a little uneasy, as though caught red-handed, but continuing to look at the charts nevertheless, defiantly, as if to show he takes orders from no one, as if busy trying to make out some underlying principle there. At last he retreats, comes over to them, looks down benignantly at their chessboard, stands there. A long silence.

"What's the range of these missiles?" he asks softly.

And they, evidently familiar with the question—

"Depends on your target."

"No, I mean . . . just like that . . . without any target . . ."

"Without a target?"

And he smiles to himself, gives it up, goes on watching the game; then off again, back to the charts, tries estimating their scale himself.

And then the OC bursts into the room: a tall young officer, skullcapped, good-looking, one of those boy-soldiers, lords of the front line, who rush about the trenches always in a hurry, never sporting their ranks; comes in and finds a dark, silent, square-set civilian puffing a pipe before the telltale charts, his fingers roving about Sudan.

"Yes?"—laying a hard hand on his shoulder.

"I'm the lecturer . . ." says the lecturer, grabbing the officer's hand and shaking it.

"Do we have a lecture tonight?" the officer exclaims, turning to the two sergeants questioningly, then dropping into a chair by the table.

But the pair of them just shrug their shoulders and animatedly swop knights.

The lecturer, ill at ease, draws on his pipe.

"Who brought him?"

"Ginger did," says one of the men with a knowing little grin at his fellow, and the lecturer sees the mischievous twinkle in the officer's eye.

"Ginger? Where is she?"

"Went to see about the movie. . . . Probably looking for you."

The officer seems flustered, picks up a short stick and begins to play with it.

"These past weeks," he tells the lecturer as if in apology, "we're simply being bombarded with lecturers, and they don't even bother to warn us ahead. . . ."

"We can drop it . . . as far as I'm concerned. . . ."

"No, why? We'll fix something. . . . What do you talk about?"

And once again the lecturer, feeling a fool, starts carefully spreading his wares. Something about the situation of our universities, or maybe the Israeli's self-image, or, say, Zionism versus the New Left. He might get some argument going. Or let the men choose, let them ask questions . . . anything . . .

The two chess players bow their heads. The officer listens, reveals some surprise, ponders.

"Pity you can't talk on some other subject . . . drugs, for instance. . . . We had a lecturer here not long ago who did. Men were fascinated. What was he called?"

But neither of the two remembers his name, only that he'd really been great. He'd shown them samples of drugs, had burnt a bit of hash here, on this table, given them a sniff too.

"Yes . . . so I've been told . . ." says the lecturer at last, in a cold fury, controlling it. "Sorry, but I'm no expert on drugs. . . ."

A silence follows, and for a split second it again seems to the lecturer that night hasn't come yet, that the sky is still blue outside, a sweet clear summer sky.

"The color of these windows . . ." he says, "so strange . . ."

But the officer sees nothing strange about it. Inspiration has come to him and he is taking charge:

"Had supper? No. Then go and grab something. Don't worry, I'll see you get yourself an audience that'll listen to anything you may say."

And he sends the lecturer back into the night, and himself returns to chase the two chess players off his bed.

11

And descending the hill, on the way to mess, alone again, he takes stock of his surroundings, gazes at the missile pits, the radar scanners, the bunker entrances, the huge generators. And as he walks he meets a steady stream of soldiers coming toward him, and knows they will presently gather to hear him, and feels again the tiny thrill of anticipation. And the farther he goes the more people swarm about him—walking, standing about in groups. He looks out for the redhead, his lost pillar of fire, stops now and then at the sound of laughter. For a moment he imagines seeing her, a flash in the center of a merry crowd, but when he goes over to ask after the mess hall he discovers only a little ginger-headed soldier talking and gesturing, cracking jokes.

A bus is parked in front of the mess hall, and a newly arrived batch of reserve soldiers wander about in their sloppy fatigues, with their outdated rifles, gather to arrange the watch, are already plotting ways to wangle a pass. And the mess is completely deserted, the tables bare, supper over. A graying, tired-faced cook serves him a meal of infantine food—a soft-boiled egg, cocoa, and porridge. As always, he devours his food rapidly, hungrily, the used dishes being cleared away as he eats, crumbs swept up around him.

He gets up still hungry, seeks to wash away the bitter taste in his mouth with something sweet, inquires after the canteen, goes and buys some chocolate wafers, a packet of razor blades which he puts in his pocket, starts peeling the first wafer out of its wrapper as he leaves, and drifts slowly back uphill, munching. Three gray-haired reserve soldiers in cartridge belts and steel helmets stop him, wave check lists in his face.

"You . . ." they demand, "when's your watch?"

He smiles:

"I'm not one of you people."

"What do you mean?"

"I mean you're wrong. I didn't come with you."

But they refuse to let go.

"Aren't you here on reserves?"

"Not with you, though. I'm here to give a lecture."

"A lecture? What about?"

But he remains silent.

"What do you lecture about?" they press him, disappointed, cheated out of a guard.

But he does not answer, studies the three crumpled, agitated figures in silence, does not answer.

And they wait, they still haven't grasped that he does not intend to answer them, but he is on his way already, up the slope between radar station and missile base, eating his wafers one by one, leaving a trail of tinfoil wrappings behind him in the dark, licking his chocolate-smeared fingers. Solitary—he has become a solitary of late, has fallen into the solitary's ways. He has started going to the cinema alone, has been caught talking to himself at traffic lights, to the amusement of people in nearby cars. Slowly he climbs on under the clear star-freckled sky, stops from time to time to peer at the missile pits, inspect them; the staleness of it, the hollowness, the tedium, the imminent divorce, the lone, onanistic nights, the child being ground down between them. And suddenly making up his mind, casting a swift glance to ensure he is unobserved, he slips down into one of the pits to feel the missiles with his own hands. And there they are, pointed at the light horizon, stolid, their color a rosy pink. Cautiously he touches them, smooths their flanks, is amazed to find them rather slippery, damp, as though covered in a fine film of oil or dew. He lifts a hand to the slender cone, takes hold of the fins. Such poised might. He squats and by the veiled starlight reads the numbers and letters inscribed on them, gently caresses the dark tangle of wires descending to the pad. And all at once a low buzz sounds and the entire platform with all of its five missiles stirs suddenly, veers left toward him as if to strike him. Hurriedly he flattens himself against the wall of the pit, ready to dig into it if need be, but the platform lets go of him, swivels blindly to the right, then finally erects itself, aims upward, and stops. The buzzing lasts another few seconds and ceases. Someone is operating the missiles from afar, pointing them straight at the sky as if he meant to fire at the stars.

He picks up the fallen briefcase, climbs out pale and shaken, meets two soldiers coming down the road who look startled at the sight of a briefcase-carrying civilian emerging from a missile pit. They halt, wait for him to come up with them, grimy, his hands besmirched with missile oil.

"Who're you?" They bar his way, suddenly assuming authority, very serious.

"I'm here to give a lecture . . ." he answers, putting on a frank air, a smiling face, suppressing his agitation.

"What were you looking for down there?"

"Nothing . . . just wanted to see what they look like from nearby. . . ."

"They might have sent you sky-high, you know. . . ."

But that is just what I wish, he wants to tell them. His lips only turn up in a wry smile, however, and he resumes his casual walk, not to excite suspicion; saunters off to inspect other missile pits, lingers here and there, and the two soldiers stay where they are, follow him with their eyes. Gradually he quickens his pace, falls straight into the hands of the officer and the girl who are waiting for him in the darkness.

"Had supper?" they ask anxiously, as if that were what he'd come to Sinai for. "Come on then, they're waiting for you. . . ."

And the lecturer gives himself up to them, follows the officer down steep, narrow steps underground, tiny, star-like lamps brushing his hair.

"Duck! . . ." He hears the officer's voice from the depth below him, and he bends his head a little and hits it hard against the ceiling.

A sharp pain stabs him. Gasping, he doubles up on the stairs, head in hands, his eyes filling with tears.

The officer turns, comes back to him, amusement in his voice.

"You too? Every damn lecturer has got to bang his head here. What's the matter with you fellows?"

But he is incapable of replying, chokes on the words, continues the descent at a stoop and enters the bunker, bowing. The place is awash with a purplish light and there are instruments everywhere—a radar screen, control panels, a small computer, sticks, levers, phones, wires, cables—all of it painted a greenish khaki. A low buzzing sounds from one corner.

"Here's your lecturer."

There are only four men in the room—one at the wireless wearing a headphone, the same two chess players still at their game on a camp bed against the wall, and one other soldier, a dull, dumb face.

"Is this all?" the lecturer asks with a little laugh. He has never had such a small audience before.

"This is it."

"Aren't you staying?"

"No . . . I've got to go. . . ."

"And that girl . . ."—in despair.

"She'll come and fetch you after. You two there, break it up. . . ."

One of the players freezes in mid-move.

"What's your subject?" asks the officer, but doesn't wait for a reply. "You tell them . . ."—and is gone.

So the moment has arrived. To break the silence at long last, to start speaking. A dull ache throbs in his head. He has waited for this moment all day, has been brought from afar for its sake. Slowly he pulls the notes out of his briefcase, biding his time. Even though it's ridiculous to stand here in this dim mudhole with four soldiers for audience and hold notes in his hand, as if he even needed them, as if he couldn't talk fluently, almost unconsciously, abandoning himself to the sweetness of his own voice, swayed by his own surreptitious, inescapable rhetoric, its slant of distortion growing as he proceeds.

The four of them watch him calmly, wordlessly, no doubt used to having a lecturer drop on them from time to time, here, between their beds, among the instruments.

Where to begin? Try something entirely new perhaps? Question them a bit about themselves. Personal questions: Who are they? What are they? How long have they to serve still? What are their plans after? Start perhaps precisely with that dumb one, who has a touch of violence about him, who needs a little sympathy perhaps, a kind word.

He takes the chair and places it in front of him, removes his watch, unbuttons his jacket, drops into the inevitable lecturer's mannerisms; rubs his hands, plans to open quietly, in a hush, now, the first phrases already welling up in him, not bearing on anything definite yet, only in due course edging toward one or another subject. What will it be this time? Perhaps the face of Israeli society in drawn-out struggle—a harsh political analysis which suddenly, toward the end, for no good reason, takes an optimistic turn. But then the lecturer catches sight of his own face on the radar screen, like a target in the grid of thin white numbered lines covering the area. Sunken eyes, a face drawn with fatigue, a mass of hair, and blood on his forehead. So there's blood. That's why the pain persists. He touches his forehead lightly, smiles at the dumb soldier. What time is it?

"Can I have some water? . . ."

The dumb one holds out a canteen.

He pours a little water over his head, then drinks some. The water soaks into the earth at his feet. He shivers a little. This silence of theirs. He approaches the instruments, smiling pleasantly. A large switch protruding from the board attracts his attention.

"What's this for?" He points at it as if it were the only one whose function he didn't know.

"To light this here up," the dumb one answers patiently, the only one of the four to respond.

"Light it up?" The lecturer sounds puzzled, unbelieving. "Can I?" And he pulls the switch all the way, secretly expecting a distant explosion, but all that happens is a row of little bulbs lighting up on the instrument panel. He turns them off. Emboldened by this apparent liberty to touch the instruments, his hand roves on, questing.

"Which . . . which one fires the missiles?"

"Why d'you want to know?"

"Nothing . . . just to see which button's pushed . . ."

"There's no such button . . . you don't exactly push anything either. . . ."

He looks straight into the soldier's blank eyes. Is he being had? He moves back to his papers which have slipped to the floor. Here, in a bunker deep underground, in the middle of the desert, he stands opposite four soldiers and is supposed to speak to them, enliven the boredom of their long days, offer some information, possibly some ideology, best of all some faith. In short—inspire them; in return for which he is exempt from guard duty.

And now he decides to begin. There is no avoiding it any longer—he'll have to give this lecture, come what may. The entire pointless, wasted day drops off him as an empty shell. Softly he embarks on the opening words. And at the same moment the signaler, too, starts speaking quietly into the mouthpiece attached around his neck; looking at the lecturer and talking to some distant person, who answers him now, who in a crisp voice reports the weather forecast, the wind force, visibility, his voice coming from a small loudspeaker fixed to the wall. And everybody strains to listen, while the signaler takes it all down in writing.

And with the return of silence the lecturer moves hesitantly back to the instruments, his embittered smile on his face.

"Can one get Tel Aviv on this too? . . ."

"Now?"

"If I may, just for a moment . . ."

The signaler rises, removes his headset, puts it over the lecturer's head, and instants later the phone is ringing at home, and the child picks it up again and his voice is clear and warm and close as if he were within arm's reach.

"Daddy's away, Mummy's asleep," he says mechanically even before being asked.

"Yorami, this *is* Daddy. . . ."

And now the child does hear him.

"Daddy?"

"Yes, this is Daddy here. Isn't Mummy up yet?"

"No."

"Then wake her up. Go wake her up right away, you hear me?"

"Yes."

But the child doesn't go, doesn't want to relinquish the phone, his breaths verging on sobs.

"Yorami . . ." he whispers anxiously. The soldiers' faces are lifted up at him, following the conversation. He fondles the switches in front of him with both his free hands.

"What are you doing now?"

"Nothing."

"Have you eaten?"

"No."

"I'll be home soon."

"Daddy? . . ."

"Yes."

And all at once the child breaks down, cries from the depths of his abandonment, unable to stop; dry, harsh wails, rising and swelling without interruption; and the men in the room with him smile a little, and only then he remembers they can hear it all over the loudspeaker, and he removes the weeping headset, casts about vainly, not knowing how to break the connection, till the signaler comes to his rescue and slowly the weeping recedes.

And all of a sudden he feels relieved. He abandons the idea of a lecture, collects his notes, replaces the watch on his wrist, makes to say something and changes his mind at once. Not a word will he utter. The chess players watch him briefly, quizzically, then start moving the few pieces still left on the board. The signaler picks up a screwdriver and starts taking the mouthpiece apart. Only the dumb soldier continues to stare at him, but the lecturer avoids his eyes, rummages through his briefcase, pulls out the volume of poetry received this morning, sits down, begins to read, barely taking in the shape of the letters, overcome by boredom. He is familiar enough with this clever-clever romanticism—sentimental stuff notwithstanding the ragged lines. He reads on all the same, turns the pages over wearily, his eyes almost shut. Ought to get the divorce, start a new life.

And still the dumb soldier's eyes haven't left his face. Is he still looking to him for a lecture, a revelation? He applies himself to the poems, skimming pages unhopefully; suddenly finds a wonderful poem, knows it to be so from the first line that is like a blow on the head. He reads quickly, once, then again. Three simple, lucid stanzas, each word in place, pearls on a dunghill. Maybe the fellow's pinched it from someone else? He reads it once more, then a fourth time, and it's as if it was meant for him personally. One more time he reads it, then looks up. The men in the bunker appear blurred, as if seen through a fog. And the radar screen in front of him fills with white scurrying dots, like a rash, like an air attack.

"There's something here . . ." he wishes to say to them, but no one is looking at him, each is intent on his own. Even the dumb soldier has despaired of him, has pulled a cheap paperback out of his pocket and sits reading it, his lips parted in excitement.

12

And at eight a shadow falls across him. The redhead stands in the doorway, has approached without making a sound and stands there tranquilly, a submachine gun over her shoulder, gazes at him seated there in the middle of the bunker, head bowed, the poetry volume on the floor at his feet.

"Finished?" she asks gently.

He makes no reply but gets up at once, stuffs the book into the briefcase, and without a word to the men in the room follows her up the steps, feeling his way, bent over, careful, but even so fully expecting to bump his head again, except that this time she waits for him beside the obstacle, lays a warm hand on the top of his head, presses it down low.

And then he is up the hill again, near the almost savage-sounding rumble of the generators, is signing a form which the skullcapped officer hands him, is looking stunned and bewildered, his clothes rumpled as though he had slept in them. Ah well, as long as he's *been* here. And a flickering light in one of the barracks reveals the audience they have deprived him of. Dozens of soldiers crowded into a smoke-filled room, absorbed in the movie he has brought. And he wants to lash out at these two here, but under his eyes she approaches the officer, kisses him, and the officer recoils slightly.

And then they are rolling down the slope, and the metal hissing under their wheels becomes earth again, the missiles and radar scanners are wiped out by the darkness as if they had never been. And the guard has changed at the gate too, and it is by elderly soldiers that they are stopped this time. The jeep escaping to freedom rouses their envy and they try to detain it, shine their flashlights into it, take down numbers, inspect papers; gray-haired, wrinkled, they fill in some form with stubborn zeal, gape at the redheaded girl behind the wheel, wink at him, and at last, reluctantly, raise the barrier.

And then they are on the arrow-straight road again, and he looks back and the missile hill is gone, only a red pinpoint floats high on a vanished aerial. And he is well content to have things dissolve like that, fade swiftly behind him. He looks at the silent girl by his side who strains over the wheel, intent on her driving, the submachine gun in her lap, her face illuminated by the glow of the headlights cast back from the road. A pale relic from another existence.

He reaches out and lightly touches her thigh.

"That hill"—he waves a hand at the dark landscape—"have we passed it yet?"

"No . . ." she smiles, and soon to his surprise the jeep leaves the road once more, and with the familiar sweep, without slowing down, starts the ascent.

13

And again he trails behind her, climbing rocks, wandering through small crevices, stumbling over rusty containers, tangles of canvas. By the feeble starlight he discerns the smashed munition crates, breathes the cool desert air, sees the land opening out to the coasts of Egypt, the distant Canal which even now, in the darkness, still glows with a faint incandescence.

How could he ever have forgotten this place? How come he hadn't recognized this rocky hill at once? This is where they had dropped him. He remembers it perfectly now. It had been on the fourth day of the Sinai campaign, at night. The chief battles were virtually over, the war decided, and they had been spending all four days at a small airfield, sitting around beside an old World War II Dakota plane. On constant alert, cut off from events, disgusted at missing what seemed from afar like a grand adventure, they lounged on the asphalt at the edge of the landing strip, under the blades of the propeller, and once every few hours or so people would come and bring them yet one more machine gun, another munition crate, an intercom set, a stretcher. Their load grew bulkier and more cumbersome day by day, till, toward dusk of the fourth evening, they were put on the plane which had suddenly come alive, and after a two-hour flight were dumped as a couple of live bundles of equipment in the no-man's-land between the two armies. A soft eastern breeze had carried them gently to this hill. At first they had tried to dig themselves in, then had just sat and waited tensely, shivering with cold, for the advancing troops. Toward dawn they had come under heavy fire from the very unit they were expecting. It took several minutes till contact was made and the shooting stopped. One of them was killed. Presently the riflemen arrived in person, gay and noisy, drunk with their swift advance through the vanquished desert. They took away the supplies and munitions, bundled him into a jeep with the dead body and sent him back to the rear. For a long time after he had still gone around feeling cheated.

"How did the lecture go?" She is standing a few paces away from him with her gun, watches his excited prowling among the rocks.

He stops, looks at her.

"The lecture?" He grins a little as if in recollection. "There wasn't any after all . . . I kept silent. . . ."

"You did, did you?"

"Yes, why not? I'm sure my predecessors said all there was to say. What more could I add?"

She laughs, appears relieved.

He approaches her.

"I mean, what's the point? Just talk for the sake of talking? Invent fake problems? Even though I could have . . ."

And suddenly he slumps on a rock at her feet, knocks his pipe out on a stone, sick at heart, stubborn.

"And I thought you'd fallen asleep," she says.

He doesn't answer. It's as if a dam had burst in him. Hands thrown wide he touches a bush, bits of fabric, metal scraps; lies back among the shapeless debris around him, lowers his head carefully to the ground, looks at the rapid motion of the sky which is growing bleary behind a thin mist. Above him the ugly freckled face with the red crown of thorns. The sadness of it. He closes his eyes.

"This lecturer ought to be buried . . . mustn't leave him lying like that . . . there aren't going to be any more wars here. . . ."

"Are you sure?" she says mockingly.

"I've seen the vast power . . . touched the missiles . . . Who could ever break through? . . ."

"We ought to get moving . . ." he hears her say.

But he doesn't want to move, he digs in, clings to the last of his liberty, is ready to stay the night in the desert, perhaps even deliver the missed lecture. And she—even his name she does not know.

But she doesn't care about his undelivered lecture, she wants to get rid of him, approaches the prostrate lecturer, touches him, tries to raise him, and he, as in a dream, bends and kisses her large foot, white sapphire no longer immaculate to his lips but filthy, filling his mouth with sand. And now she recoils, tries to shake him off, drags him along the ground a pace, pulls him up, and he feels the power in her, in her strong hands.

"You'll miss your plane. . . ."

14

The steps are all but dropped away under his feet, and he has no sooner got on the plane than it starts to roll as if his boarding had set it in motion. And once again he is the only civilian, and the soldiers, bareheaded and well behaved, sit quietly rustling their papers, not even glancing at the latecomer. And he sinks at once on a vacant seat in the rear, fastens the seat belt, watches the torches disappear on the runway one by one, and is already growing bored again, jumps up in his everlasting restlessness to find someone to sit by. And toward the front he discovers the gray head of the battery-commander he talked to a few hours ago at the service base. He slips in beside him with a nod and a smile, but the colonel fails to recognize him, reads on, in the same manual still, with the same absorption. The lecturer waits awhile, then lays a tentative hand on the colonel's shoulder. The other starts.

"You don't remember me. I'm the lecturer."

"What lecturer?"

"At the battery–612."

The man removes his glasses, stares at him as if he were seeing a ghost.

"You? . . . You got back from there? . . ."

"Yes . . ."

"And they listened to you?"

"Certainly. In perfect silence. I had a hard time getting them to let me go."

"You're lucky. They're pretty tough with lecturers as a rule."

"Not with me, though. They were wonderful. Showed me the view, took me to the missile pits, spread out charts, showed me around the control rooms, the instruments, the radar, everything . . . explained how things worked . . . I nearly fired a missile myself. . . ."

The colonel seems bothered, frowns. The lecturer's hands, which are black with oil, the mud on his clothes, his flushed face and the blood on his forehead, and on top of that the shrill note that has crept into his voice—

"A wonderful experience to see that vast might . . . and the perfect camouflage . . . not a pinpoint of light . . ."

And beyond the window, between sky and dark desert, he suddenly discovers himself, sailing serenely through space, his features heavy, weary, the day-old stubble like a grayish vapor on his cheeks, stars entwined in his hair.

"There's just one thing I didn't quite get"—still clinging to the elderly officer—"what depth do these missiles reach? . . ."

"What range, you mean."

"Range. Of course: range."

"Depends what exactly you're aiming at."

"The maximum . . ." says the lecturer with sudden heat.

But the colonel waxes impatient:

"No. What it is you want to hit."

"No, I mean—just at random . . . not to hit anything."

"If it's not to hit, you don't fire."

The lecturer bows his head. No chance they'll ever understand him. And meanwhile the colonel is already engaged in getting rid of him, puts his glasses back on, returns to the manual and becomes engrossed in it again. And down below lights spring up from the emptiness, more and more lights. Signs of habitation, villages, lamplit roads, intersections, light upon light; and then there is the sea, and the shore, and Tel Aviv coming up at them.

And the doors open, everyone getting up, and the colonel swiftly escaping from him; and he is the last to step off the plane and finds it is raining outside. A spring rain is sweeping the town. And all at once he is reluctant to go home, wanders a little about the wet, deserted airfield, turns to the emptying terminal and finds a telephone under a leaking booth top, rain slanting in at him.

"It's me," he tells his wife who picks up the receiver, "you hear me?"

"Yes."

And again, the chill—

"What happened? Where's the kid?"

"Asleep."

"Managed to wake you up finally, did he? . . ."

"No . . . I found him asleep in front of the television set."

The child wandering about by himself all afternoon. In the end they'll kill him between them.

"What happened? What happened to you?" he flares up, rain lashing at him, a headache starting.

"What do you want now? . . ."

Her remoteness, her loathing.

"I've been in Sinai, at a missile base. I rang up several times. What happened to you? What made you sleep like that? Nearly all day . . ."

She remains silent.

"You hear me?" his voice softening all at once.

"Yes."

"Look, is something the matter?"

"What's it to you?"

This endless privation, the unchanging hostility. Perhaps she even attempted suicide. So the war's still on. Whereas he would suddenly be willing to yield, to forgive. The headache mounts. The dead pipe in his hand drips wetly. He sways a little under the leaking roof. But he will go home prepared to give battle.

The Last Commander

The Gnostics, who were the contemporaries of the Jewish Tannaim of the second century, believed that it was necessary to distinguish between a good but hidden God who alone was worthy of being worshipped by the elect, and a Demiurge or creator of the physical universe, whom they identified with the "just" God of the Old Testament.

GERSHOM SCHOLEM
"Redemption Through Sin"

CHAPTER I

After the war there we were in murky offices, pushing pencils, and sending form letters to one another on matters which seemed important to us. Had we lost, we would have been in a real mess now. We would have been accounting for murder, for robbery, committed by our dead comrades. Since we had won—we brought liberation, but they had to give us something to do, otherwise nobody would vacate the fast, murderous jeeps, full of machine guns and rounds of ammunition.

Now our clothes are clean; no grime on our faces. Only adding machines are softly humming at our side, and at night, in the crazy city, we rush from place to place to avoid loneliness. We run from light to light, clinging to our jaded women. Our eyes grow weak.

Each year when summer comes around, the reservists go off for military practice. The commands flutter around the offices like white soft bullets, but they don't touch us—the veterans. At first we felt slighted, but we consoled ourselves: no doubt this world needs us and our sharp pencils. Seven years we fought without stopping. Our nights have become hollow with fear. Now they ask us to rest on our withered laurel wreaths. So we barricaded ourselves behind piles of letters.

But this year when summer came around, strange to say, we too were caught. Our good brothers, the officers in charge of sending out the summonses, remembered us. And the call-up summonses landed on our desks to our amazement. No escape.

One fine day they loaded us dodgers, former military men, onto freight cars, and sent us off to the south, to clamber up the hills.

And now, who knows, we might have picked up the weapons—unfamiliar to our hands by now, and run away and stormed off; carried packs and fought until our strength gave out in new, imagined battles; attacked, retreated, returning again to conquer the wind and ourselves—had it not been for Yagnon—a swarthy, angular character, who was appointed at the last moment and with some trepidation to substitute for the commander of the company who was suddenly called away on some business.

Already at the point of departure near the desert crossroads we could see that the new commander tarried. While the rest of the companies were very busily engaged in loading equipment to go off to some place of action and trouble, and the commanders were running back and forth, this one went up on a small hill at the side of the road, and there he dozed off all by himself, bared to the sun. I remember our men hanging around idly by the silent machines—grunting and grumbling. The other companies disappeared one by one, and the square quieted down. But that black dot on top of the hill didn't move. No one knew the reason for this delay. Fed up with one another, scorched by the heat, we hadn't yet realized that from now on time was not our own. Darzi and Hilmi, two division commanders, approached me, their limbs moving restlessly. In the war they had served as sappers, and they had blown up whole villages along with their inhabitants, and since then they don't move without one another, out of fear.

I could see that the hours were passing, so I climbed up the hill and went over to him. This was the first time that I really saw him. He was lying at my feet—an elongated form with limbs stretched out, sporting a huge broken nose in an ugly face. With bifocals perched on his eyes and a long scar deeply imprinted on his forehead. He was sleeping in a state of deep fatigue, but his breathing was barely audible. I knew that he, too, had served in the lower echelon in one of the offices, but he was a bachelor, and in the war he had displayed bold leadership on the southern front. I bent over and touched him. I remember his look—tear-veiled from sleeping in the sun. If death is very close to life, then death had been caught in his eyes. He lifted his head slowly, calmly, like one who had an eternity of them. An old khaki shirt hung limply on his body. No military stripes.

"The other units have already left," I said, bending over him. "Isn't it time for us?"

He shot me a look out of another world.

"What?" His lips broke out in a strange drawl.

I repeated what I had said.

A weak smile lit up his mouth.

"You're in a hurry?" he said in a kind of mocking surprise.

Only when the heat subsided and a breeze came up from the desert did he bestir himself, glided weakly down the hill, got up on an old bullet-ridden jeep which had been given us, a survivor of the war years. The whole column followed in his footsteps.

We traveled for many hours, slowly, with long stops. It seemed as though lead had been poured into the wheels of the cars that were crookedly wending their way at the bidding of the drowsy officer. We pressed deeper and deeper into the heart of the desert, getting ever farther away from any shadow of a settlement. Nobody knew where we were going. In the north, we had fought for every house, for every clod of earth; but in this desert only a few scattered small units were roaming about, without direction and without reason. The whole wide expanse was conquered in a swift, seven-day campaign. Anything wider than a narrow parcel of dust cutting through the length of the desert was beyond our ken.

The sun beat down on the cars that wormed their way around in the menacing chalk-white region, somberly, through sand dunes glistening with fool's gold, oceans of wasteland whose gentleness belied the eye. In the evening we found ourselves ascending a strange mountain, a formidable reddish ridge of Hymettian stone and reddish-black rocks. The wheels of the cars were caught in the steep rise little by little, until finally the sputtering motors gave out and stalled in the middle of their ascent, halfway up the mountain, next to a wide, deep rut with desert brush sticking out of it, their branches twisted as though demented.

We jumped out of the cars, weakened and confused, and a dim, ghostlike twilight encircled us. The drivers unloaded the cases of army rations, unfastened the trailing water tank, and disappeared to the rear down the slope. Like sleepwalkers we began going around among the piles of equipment that were thrown around, among the heaped weapons, coming to a halt and standing at the mouth of the abyss that was but a chain of extinct volcanic craters; their bases were either cooled off or still smoldering. Every step opened up long and gaping canyons, small craters that dropped—crookedly—to deep layers of chalk, broken up in a mysterious way. We were still wandering about when the officer who looked now like a dark brown hawk went into the rut, spread out a blanket for himself on the ground, curled up, and without a word, fell asleep. We were still bunched together here and there, looking for food, but the utter chaos confused everything. One after another we followed him into the rut, hungry and tired. Soon all had fallen asleep around the new officer, after a day in which nothing was accomplished.

Until late in the morning the camp was asleep and silent. The slow crawling rays of the sun added slumber to slumber. A strange, paralyzing heat flowed beneath us all the time, from hidden sources in the mountain itself, as if we had been placed inside a giant furnace. Darzi and Hilmi crept over to me, drowsily and heavily, and snuggled up next to me, among the smoldering rocks. From their mumbling I figured out that they wanted to know whether to awaken the men, since the new officer didn't seem to show any signs of life.

The heat of the sun was now more intense and there was a burning sensation which weakened everybody. From between the slits of our aching eyes, the rocks looked like trembling molluscs, formations of sandstone running amok in a riot of colors. The blue of sky disappeared and in its place there remained only a stark white heat. No soldier moved a muscle. Here and there somebody would try to move around, but immediately his legs would buckle and collapse to the ground. Only the youngest among us, the commander of the fourth unit, an officer of the youth corps, who at the time of the war was still a child and collected bags of bullets, he alone got up and wandered around, ready for a day's work. He glanced apprehensively at his slumbering commander, then he settled at the edge of the abyss, and cleaned his weapons.

The morning hours passed. The bellies of the soldiers of the division stretched out around me were glued to the ground. At noon Yagnon suddenly turned over from one side to the other, opened his eyes and gazed at the world while lying on his back, took a cigarette from his shirt pocket, and lit it. The whole camp lay in wait for his every move. We got up bent over and came near him; the youth joined us. We knelt, all together, at the side of the officer, who tossed his ugly head in our direction.

"What's to be done today?" the young officer burst out. Yagnon didn't answer. A queer grimace twisted his mouth. The scar on his forehead was gleaming like a long, bloody stain.

"Today," repeated the youth, almost angrily, "what's to be done today?"

Yagnon didn't move from his place. His slim, tanned hand was thrown over his sack, between his mussed-up blankets. Papers rustled. A smile came over his lips.

"There are plans," he whispered tiredly. "They gave me plans," he repeated.

The young man tried to seize the practice plans.

"So then what's to be done today? One just can't keep on crouching like this."

He was aflame with the heat, and it seemed that he was right.

The tiny eyes of Yagnon glided along Hilmi and Darzi's palpitating bellies, lying crisscrossed, at least that is the way I saw them. His lips mumbled drowsily.

"Today—rest . . . at night perhaps . . . the heat will subside . . . now—rest."

Darzi bent his head toward the figure bundled up on the ground.

"Rest," he repeated with an inward smile.

We looked at each other, all three of us. The young officer wanted to open his mouth, but we had already disappeared, stooping down over the rim of the shadow under the scrawny trees, returning to the sweaty slumber. When the heat subsided, when it started to get dark, Yagnon again woke up, and sucked on a cigarette. It was clear to all of us that he was not setting aside the upcoming night for anything but sleep. Again, one after the other, we succumbed to heat-ravaged slumber, riddled with disturbing fantasies. And in the morning we were still lying down, only more tired than we were before.

On the third day we had already removed our clothes. Rank disappeared. We wondered suspiciously what schemes the sleeping man was devising. But, after the hours passed without anything doing, we knew that he had decided to lie low on the rocks until the end of the practice period.

We were struck with terror when we realized his clear, simple purpose. We attacked the deceiving shrubs, we uprooted and reduced them to splinters. We made a fire and nibbled without appetite on some dry rations we had on hand. Now there was not even a shadow of a shade.

On the fourth day, at noontime, we woke up. A hot wind whispered through the clefts of the rocks. Sun-scorched papers were flying around us, we would make a weak attempt to catch some of them. Yagnon had let fly the practice plans. The wireless was cracked, and the sleepy liaison officer had tied it with blankets, and had placed it under his head. The only possible connection with other units was severed. At twilight the young officer suddenly jumped up, got on the jeep that was left with us, to escape this hell. The roar of the engine shattered the silence. They all opened their eyes, but no one got up from his place. They hoped it would alarm and deliver the sleeping officer. The jeep started gliding down the incline; suddenly the dry brakes snapped, and it rolled down to the edge of the abyss and got stuck between two rocks. He was saved by a miracle. He returned shamefacedly to us, his eyes on fire. That night we didn't see any more of the moon and the stars. Complete darkness covered the mountain.

On the fifth day the sound of a driven car was heard in the mountains, horn blowing noisily, and its men were shooting in the air, looking for us. Perhaps letters were coming from the cold, far-off city, the memory of which had completely disappeared. Again the young man straightened up, like a roe deer—his blue eyes flustered. The sun scorched his skin, he was all aflame. He cocked his weapon, shot into space, pierced the silence. The dialogue of shots continued for a long time, but the abysses scrambled the echoes. The car kept getting farther away. He started going around among us like a madman, yelling and pleading. Drowsy and indifferent, we observed his thin shadow gliding around us. After the car had disappeared and silence was restored, he was still standing like a hurt child, his fist unclutching his weapon, until at last he sank down near Yagnon, who smiled at him tiredly. During the night he disappeared and was not seen again. Perhaps he is still lost among the craters.

We are getting confused as to the number of the days, but already the sixth day has arrived, and as our skin blackened, so has our human image faded. People who used to pray stopped praying. The six working days passed in idleness, and on the Sabbath our capacity for slumber doubled. By now we know only the rocks hanging over our heads. We are lying in a group but each one is alone. Our hearing is clearer in the silence, and when we make an attempt to speak, we whisper. Nobody is looking for us, nobody ever gets up here. At times in the winding wadi below there are what appear to be three tiny figures, swathed in black, one in front and two in the rear, in a fixed order. These are our silent, bitter, vanquished enemies, but no one wakens to the danger that it is possible to slaughter all of us with one dagger—without a single outcry.

Only occasionally, at night, would somebody's mind become lucid, and he would toss around, unable to fall asleep. He jumps up all by himself and sees the mountain very clearly with all its sharply edged outlines. He circles the sleepy camp crying softly to the sleeping men. He too feels like sleeping. When he reaches the ugly face of Yagnon he halts, he seems to think that he hears cries of pain from the neighboring mountain, into which those black-swathed ones are disappearing. With nothing else to do, he feverishly piles up rocks. Then his passion suddenly subsides, and a dry, ashen look returns to his lips. He sinks down on the spot where he is standing—and returns to forgetfulness. On the next day, in the light, between one fit of slumber and the next he discovers next to him only a pile of rocks.

For seven days we have been captives in this realm, in the power of this skinny magician who can't get enough sleep. But there is a kind of bewitching delight in having leaden legs that keep getting entangled, in the waning consciousness.

"God Almighty," a mumbling cry is heard at times—"why didn't we come here after the war?"

And at night, again and again, one dreams about the war.

CHAPTER II

Was this Sunday? We were lost in reverie when suddenly we heard a faint rumbling sound over our heads. We lifted our eyes. In the white expanse of brightness a gray dot fluttered over us. We rubbed our eyes, when a roaring, bellowing helicopter in a whirlpool of dust and wind hovered like a bird over the furrow in the earth. Suddenly its flight was arrested in mid-air, a rope ladder unfurled, bags were thrown out, and a sturdy figure descended, waved a hand to the pilots who were disappearing in flight like blue angels. Perplexed and tired, we raised our heads from the dirt. He gathered his bags and came toward us with firm strides we could no longer match. Flushed, human, heavy-framed, silver-haired, blue, paternal eyes, and hands that knew how to praise. Insignia gleamed on his shoulders. He held back for a second, surveyed the bunch of shadows that peered at him—black, lean, bare.

We gazed at him. We knew—that's our enemy.

He made a firm decision, stepped over to a soldier who had straightened up in shock, and said curtly:

"I am the company commander . . . where is my deputy?"

We led him to Yagnon, who was sleeping, as always. His heavy shadow completely covered the slim figure. We sank down by the side of the slumbering man, we touched him. He opened his small, crafty eyes.

"Yagnon," we whispered, all bent over and frightened.

The company commander measured him with his eyes, undecidedly.

"You are my deputy?"

He nodded his head as he lay on the ground. Our hearts went out to his ugly face.

"What happened? Someone killed?" The sturdy commander turned his eyes on us.

Our tongues moved without a sound. The words got choked. We are dead, we tried to tell him. But he wasn't looking for an answer. He had already stopped listening. He wiped away his sweat and spoke: "Why did you come to this furrow? I hovered in the sky for a long time looking for you . . . and it was only with difficulty that I found time to come to you . . . They say that since the end of the war you haven't done a thing."

No one blinked an eyelash. He surveyed the furrow wonderingly.

"How in the world . . . utter chaos . . . so one lies, like this, naked?"

His voice was sharp like a whip. We kept mum. Yagnon shut his eyes tiredly, his head still lying on the ground. The officer cocked his ear—demanded an answer.

"Today: rest." Darzi's voice rose at last as if from beyond the grave.

"Rest?" roared the company commander, and his roar awakened the remaining sleepers.

"Rest," uttered Hilmi naïvely and with frightened eyes, "Sabbath today?"

A threat rent the officer's mouth. Even I murmured apologetically.

"The days got mixed up."

They all nodded their heads with me. Our souls were already sold to the man who lay on his back, and gazed quietly with dead eyes.

The commander was taken aback. He was an officer of high rank, and he was not used to insolence. Even during the war they uttered his name respectfully, though he was a civilian. At that time he used to travel around the world, and he was the one who used to bring ammunition to the depleted armories. He could have been resting now in his huge office, but he always keeps looking for the main action. When he heard that they were conscripting the war heroes, the dodgers, he made himself a company commander, and if it had seemed that he would not appear, here he was.

From then on he didn't utter a sound. He bent over his bags and rummaged around in them. Solitary and strong, a white figure. He pitched a small tent outside the furrow and shut himself in it. When evening came he crept out of his tent, and roamed a bit among the piles of equipment that were thrown about until he found a broken lamp. He fixed it and lit it. For the first time we had light. All night the lamp glowed next to him and from behind the canvas of the tent his outline was silhouetted devising schemes and bent over plans.

On the following day he got us up before dawn, before light. With dictatorial anger he delivered us from the furrow, and soon we were standing before him in sleepy formation, armed and ready. The tardy ones he sent to the mountain peak to light a fire for the rising sun. He dispatched the officers to put on insignia. When the skies lit up with golden rays, and the fire died down, the tardy returned, and then we all climbed after him in a long file, with Yagnon trailing along at the end like a black shadow. We ascended and were caught in a difficult vise until we came to the mountain peak, to the blue sky that was spread out in close enormity. All day we fired into the abyss, until our shoulders were fractured with pain. In the evening we ran after him down the slope, and he did not allow us to eat or drink until we had put up a high flagpole. At night we again climbed up the mountain, under star-studded skies. Until midnight we fired in the darkness, hitting and missing, with the echoes rolling all around us. The remaining half of the night we had alternate guard duty with the commander-who-knew-no-sleep awakening the guards.

We had only slept a few hours, and here it was Tuesday, and he was standing over us—clean, alert, and cross. In the morning twilight, heavy and weak, we fell in to raise the forgotten war flag which he brought with him, and to hear the order of the day which he composed, a biblical psalm. All that day we dug ditches, camp sites, and pits. Our hands were blistered, as though leprous. There was no rest. From trench to trench he passed, and upbraided the lazy ones. Our eyes searched desperately for Yagnon, but he—work of the devil—found himself a deep pit and slept on from the war days, and while we were striking the rocks in vain he was swallowed up in his pit, and dozed off. Smoke from his cigarette curled up from time to time. At evening we dug out holes for lavatories, we covered them with tin, and gathered our scattered excretions into one place. From now on we walk to the edge of the canyon to relieve ourselves. With the setting rays licking the burning rocks, he was the first to go there. The whole company hung around feebly, icy eyes glued to the sturdy figure crouched over there by itself.

At night—a bonfire. He assembled us in circles and talked about the war. About the war that was, about the war that will be. Is there ever a moment without a war? Is there ever rest? He stood before us and read from the book of wars, in a clear, flat voice, as though giving orders. Our heads were nodding and drooping, but he shot pebbles at the dozers and kept them jumping. As midnight approached he demanded all of a sudden that we sing the battle songs that had long since sunk into oblivion. We looked at one another fearfully, as if we were having a nightmare. But he kept right after us. We sang. Hesitating at first, hoarse, but little by little our singing turned unto a terrible wail, drunken and wild. Exhausted from a burning hot day of toil, we yelled and bellowed out the old bloody battle songs. He was standing, arms crossed over his heart, a trace of a smile on his lips. After which he turned serious, silenced us by raising a firm hand, and sent us off to our blankets, to our guard duties. There will be a big day tomorrow, he said.

And on Wednesday we charged. The whole art of fighting that we had forgotten came back to us in one day. From hill to hill, from mount to mount, he collected us and showed us where to charge, where to win. Afterward we would spread out on the rocky hills, running, shooting, and falling until winning as he said. At noon, when we had been running in the wadi, and our eyes were blurred with the heat and dust, there appeared before us a short distance away the three figures clad in black. We stopped for a moment, gazing, but the roaring commander, who was running after us with his helmet falling over his hot face, noticed them, cocked his gun, and fired at them. And immediately they disappeared light and swift into one of the canyons, like a mirage.

Where is Yagnon?

At times it seems to us that we see him treading soundlessly at the side of the commander, a dark, shadowy figure. But mostly he would appear to be going around alone in the mountain chains. The commander could keep the whole company under control by himself, and it seemed that he was afraid of his strange adjutant, the tired officer, who throughout the war was busy with the dead.

In the evening, in a period of slight rest, the commander busied himself with a car. He was wonderfully capable and he fixed it right away. At night its two headlights shone, strange, large lights. The whole night we charged back and forth within the beams of the light that it threw over the surrounding hills. Terror gripped us again. The smell of sulphur that stuck to our clothes brought the war back to us. The morning chill found us at the foot of the mountain, fainting with fatigue, but still alert enough to hear with the last ounce of strength his comments on the methods of a war that he had never fought. At dawn we returned to the deserted furrow, to the flag, after a sleepless night. He fixed his blue eyes upon us, smiled to himself, and said: "It's Thursday."

In the morning a new drill was set up. He stood on top of the mountain, and it was up to us to reach him, without being noticed. The whole mountain was full of soldiers crawling like insects, trying to hide from him. It was hopelessly impossible. Whenever we thought we had gotten to the top and reached him, his alert eyes would trip us in time, and turn us back again to the starting point, to the place where Yagnon was lying, smiling and blowing clouds of smoke. Before this we had intended to fall asleep in one of the passes between the great rocks, but since yesterday we hadn't had a drop of water in our mouths, and the water was beside him who was on top of the mountain. Crazed with thirst, we were creeping, scratched and dry, until noontime. No one succeeded in reaching him. He won.

In the afternoon, no one paid any attention to the sound of the car wandering around the mountains, carrying letters. But he heard. He assembled us at once and commanded us to go and meet it. We marched a great distance and found it stuck in one of the small wadis. We freed its wheels from the pits, we cleared the path before it, we split rocks, and as a reward we received crumpled and yellowed letters from those who remained in the city. They wrote us about their petty worries. We wanted to throw the letters away. He stood there and demanded of all of us that we send our answers, as in the war days, so that they would know that we were still living, and wouldn't mourn. We leaned over and scrawled large letters on top of the rocks, staring at him with open hostility. We returned to the camp in a trot around the mountain.

On Friday he was feeling good. He said: "I haven't done anything yet . . . I haven't accomplished half of what I want." All day he spread out and rolled up maps and colored diagrams which he had brought with him, to demonstrate to us what was going to take place, what was yet going to happen. When he saw that we were dozing off in front of him he dispatched us to pitch tents outside of the furrow, in precise squares. There will be a shade over your head, for your damned tiredness.

In the evening he instructed those who prayed to pray. Even the agnostics—it is better for them to pray, to ease their troubled minds. He stood and looked at them until their hurried prayer ended. At night he took out of his pack a box of broken, dried-up biscuits that he had brought with him, and divided them fairly and evenly with us. He was glad, so he said, that he had accomplished a great change in six days; no longer do we crouch dejectedly in the dry furrow. He rubbed his strong hands together, slowly and firmly. And isn't everything all right? We didn't answer. He doesn't really want an answer. And anyway has anybody except him said anything throughout these six days?

A gleaming night is spread over us. A strong dark sky. A deep rumble grows in the distance. The canvasses of the tent are flapping in the wind. The mess has disappeared under the precisely folded blankets. We had said: Tonight we shall rest, we shall sleep. But he did not favor that. He wanted to sum up, to give himself credit. Since the war we hadn't done anything. All night he spoke to us about the fighting man.

Sabbath. Stones in our skulls instead of eyes. Hush. Quiet. As in the days when we first came here. Now it seems that we are permitted to sleep, but we can't. We keep opening our leaden eyelids to see what he is doing. How does he relax. Does he rest? The tiny tents are suffocating us. The shade is hot and dirty, not much of a shade. We are dying to close our eyes, we must. We have had a week of terror, and another week of terror was yet to come. The hours were passing, but sleep did not come. Painfully awake, like driven dogs we groped around on the ground to find a place for ourselves.

Yagnon. We remind ourselves of that one individual deep in sleep in the deserted furrow—why has he abandoned us?

And out of the corners of inflamed eyes, against our will, we keep seeing the company commander who is making the rounds among the tents, alert and awake, smiling at our drooping faces.

"Why don't you sleep? You say you're tired. At night I hear you crying."

CHAPTER III

In the evening, at the end of the Sabbath, he assembled the officers and Yagnon in his tent in order to give directions for a taxing march of seven days' duration through the Wilderness of John and its plains, up to a distant well of water at the desert crossroads, where cars will wait for us to take us back home. All night he kept us in his tent and spelled out for us every item of the march with maddening attention to detail. Plans for assaults, charges, entrenchments, retreats, complicated night raids. With his swift red pencil he encircled on the map places where he wanted to stage battles with an imaginary enemy, and the point of his pencil cruelly indicated the many kilometers that we would be carrying the imaginary wounded. He wanted to conduct the march under military conditions, with pack and ammunition, with meager rations of food and water, without rest. He ordered us to take the tents with us, and to drag along the boxes of ammunition; so that no trace of our existence be left in the furrow.

We bit our lips in anger, looked up at Yagnon who was sucking on a cigarette in the darkness of the tent, but he didn't raise his head. We exchanged hopeless looks. Darzi took heart, extended a weak hand toward the officer, who was bent over the map, his voice wavering.

"Why the tents?" he said sarcastically. "At any rate there will be no time to fall asleep in them."

The company commander directed his blue gaze at us. Darzi was awed, waiting for the scathing anger of the commander.

"In vain . . ." Another word died on his lips. The company commander controlled his temper, but rage made his quiet voice quiver. Once more he spoke about the war that was, the war that will be. About the blood, about those who would be killed, about the crying, about the need to learn how to win. Suddenly he turned to the silent spark that was lighting one cigarette with another, as though he knew that in that one's silence lay all the trouble. Yagnon removed the cigarette from his mouth, lifted his eyebrows in mock amazement, and said in his warm, quiet voice:

"Of course these are plans."

And he put the live fire back into his mouth. The commander's eyes softened. He passed his glance over the men who were sitting bent and crushed. He knew that the march would be taxing, but was there really any other choice? Are we the masters? Years ago, in the war, battles took place here, and through the arid Plain of John men went out on offensive marches. He bent his body toward us; his eyes were glistening. Perhaps we would find remains of equipment, or even skeletons of fighters who were killed in the passes. He looked sternly into the gloomy space that was visible from behind the folds of the tent. With unconcealed sorrow. What a pity that he wouldn't be able to lead us on that march.

The last sentence that was swallowed up in the darkness made our hearts leap with sudden joy. We didn't believe what our ears had heard. Only Yagnon didn't bat an eyelash.

"You aren't going out with us?" we asked with unconcealed joy.

"No . . . I only came here for seven days . . . no more."

We lowered our heads so that he wouldn't notice the relief that engulfed us. Only slow-witted Hilmi slipped in with a delighted voice, "Who will take you, sir?"

He smiled with sovereign condescension. "Those who brought me . . . tomorrow morning."

We shook hands thankfully.

After he finished speaking, we went out of the tent. A desert breeze was blowing. Only a few hours remained before sunrise, and although we were broken up after a night of planning, we weren't looking for sleep. Hilmi and Darzi lit a small bonfire at the edge of the abyss, and the four of us sat around the fire. The heat enveloped our drowsy limbs. The star-strewn sky was hazy, and the shadows of the mountains long. From time to time we would smuggle a look at Yagnon who was sitting with us. This was the first time that he looked wide awake and his eyes were inwardly twinkling with a strange smile.

The fire attracted the company commander. He came over to say good-by to us in a nice, friendly way if we would only carry out his orders. At the edge of the abyss he stepped toward us, somewhat cautious. He came, he seated himself near us, he warmed his strong hands in the fire. The light fell on his handsome face. His eyes lifted up beyond the Plain of John, whose border points to the north, a place where the ridges end. After that he examined us with a steady gaze. No bashfulness in his eyes, no perplexity. He kept looking at Yagnon without let-up, he kept trying to tear apart the curtains that he was wrapped in. But that one kept smoking peacefully away, and his eyes kept lapping up the fire. Suddenly the commander jerked his head back, partly stating, partly asking:

"You fought here . . . in these mountains."

Yagnon raised his eyes to him. For the first time they gleamed with interest.

"Yes."

"They say that some bitter fighting took place here."

"Yes."

"Why?"

"We were surrounded."

"Surrounded?"

"Yes."

"Where?"

"Here . . . around this very mountain. We hid in this furrow . . . we were hiding."

"And after that you broke out and beat the enemy." He wasn't asking. He was stating facts.

"No . . . we fled. We escaped through the Plain of John."

"The Plain of John," we whispered.

"Yes," answered the quiet, somewhat sloven voice of Yagnon. "On the road they murdered us all. The retreat lasted seven days."

"Seven?" We recoiled.

"Seven."

At dawn the watchmen awakened the camp. The men got up in fear. Already word had leaked out about the long and tiring journey that was arranged. They packed their bags and grumbled, tied up the tents and grumbled, they removed the crates of ammunition from the pits and divided them among themselves, and the grumbling rose to the very heavens wan in the light of the dawn. They nibbled on their dry rations, formed subordinate groups, and already the packs were on their shoulders, and the polished weapons in their hands. The sun's rays that streamed from the mountain, like broken arrows, lit up the company that stood in formation laden and weighted down with iron helmets, weapons and ammunition, and with the tents rising like squashed towers from the stooped shoulders. Sixty pairs of eyes intent on evil searched for Yagnon. The commander passed in front of the soldiers, his bag in his hand. The grumblings fell like sheaves.

Seven days he was with us, and each day was branded with a hot iron. He tried to impose order, and what he brought was terror. Now he is trying to clear us out of here to bruise our feet for seven days with the rocks of the arid John wilderness. What for? Is there anything we need here? Is there anything we search for here? The ugly vulture, the corpse, spread out here. He didn't demand a thing. We are tired. We have gazed open-eyed into the abyss. The sun has scorched us.

The commander spoke to the soldiers, described the way, talked about the drills. If we should complete the journey before seven days we could return to our homes earlier. His smile lit up his face. Would we indeed be strong enough to complete the difficult journey in less than seven days? No one stirred. Not a sound. He didn't even want an answer. He finished his short message, and his eyes looked for Yagnon; that one crept out of the rear of the company, saddled with a helmet, and a cane in his hand. In that same instant a faint buzzing noise was heard. They all lifted their eyes to the sky. A gray dot was moving on high.

The commander said to Yagnon, and his voice cut the air:

"Take your men and get on your way!"

Yagnon raised his dark eyes to him, but did not stir. All were glued to the maneuvering plane in the sky, looking for us. The feet stuck to the ground. If we should go down the slope we wouldn't ever come back here.

The company commander bristled with a stern look.

"What are you waiting for?" he roared at the bunch of platoon officers, who were standing at the side and were looking intently at him, petrified. They shifted unwillingly from place. The men lifted the crates of ammunition, ready to march. But the pupils of the eyes didn't budge from the plane that was getting bigger, flying like something from outer space. Suddenly Yagnon picked up his feet, marked time slowly, and came and stood in front of the commander, bending over with a sort of slight bow. The scar on his forehead looked like a dark, wide-open hole.

The commander gaped in astonishment.

"Mister"—his lips stammered out the civilian term, and his eyes narrowed—"they want to see how they're going to take you out of here . . . so that we will remember . . . please, mister . . ."

The noise of the plane turned into a frightening blast. A whirlpool of winds went wild all around us, a smarting and very fine dust covered us. The helicopter, agitated and stormy, started to come to a stop very slowly onto the ground. Now to our joy we couldn't understand a word of the shoutings of the company commander. We only saw his moving lips. A door opened in the helicopter, and a rope ladder unfurled. The pilots, wearing sun visors and earphones, smiled at us who were standing laden with arms and pack.

Yagnon poked among the rocks with his cane. Everybody is waiting in hushed silence. Only now did the company commander understand what we were planning, burdened and mum as we were. Like a madman he ran between the lines, but the awesome vehicle drowned out his voice. Tears stood in his eyes, his hands trembled all of a sudden. The pilots accelerated the noise impatiently, laughing. Strange and removed—from a blue, swift world.

He waved his fists at them, alone under the sky and on the earth, his back bowed, the first time that we saw him at a loss, helpless. He climbed the rope ladder, then stopped suddenly and turned his chiseled head to us. His lips twisted in a sort of shudder. He murmured a few quiet, mute last words. Curses. We bowed our heads. His body was swallowed up inside the helicopter which at once ascended from its place. The noise was dying down, the clouds of dust settled on the ground. The plane melted into the sky, and calm returned to the everlasting mountains.

Without a word, each man turned full circle. We unloaded the pack, the arms we threw down. We threw away the crates of ammunition. Quietly, on tiptoe, like someone walking with the fear of God, light-footed and intoxicated with the light. Spellbound we made our way to the kitchen tent and threw it to the ground, someone kicked the lamp until it fell apart. The toilets that we had put up were smashed in a twinkling, the tins were flying in the air. Two tackled the deserted flagpole and broke it in two. Everything returned to its former state, and before much time had elapsed, we were again sprawled out inside the furrow, exposed to the morning light, to the growing heat of the sun rays. Yagnon had already shut his eyes.

The horror of white heat is burning on us. The sun does not leave us alone. We are tired and we are growing wearier by the hour. We have returned to the tender mercies of Yagnon's bony hands. Many days are still left for us to sleep here.

Day after day passes. A sleepy, paralyzed camp. Only from time to time does someone of us lift his eyes to the gleaming expanse of white, which is called sky, in case a gray dot is fluttering, trying to come down to us and bring him back again.